Never Let Go

Lauren Biel

This is a work of fiction. Names, characters, events, and incidents are the products of the author's imagination. Any resemblance to actual persons, living or dead, or actual events is purely coincidental.

Paperback ISBN: 979-8-9855002-3-3

Library of Congress Cataloging-in-Publication Data

Never Let Go/Lauren Biel 1st ed.

Printed in the United States of America

Cover Design: Pretty In Ink Creations

Content Editing: Sugar Free Editing

Interior Design: Sugar Free Editing

For more information on this book and the author, visit: www.LaurenBiel.com

This book depicts adult themes and difficult situations. For a full list of content advisories, please visit www.LaurenBiel.com.

For my readers who like fucked-up shit

Chapter One

BENJAMIN

I stared out the window, cool black metal beneath my hand. The bars obscured most of my vision, but the outline of the moon peeked from behind the treetops.

"Stop stargazing and come help me," came a gruff voice from behind me. I turned my head toward the sound. Marcy peered back at me, her lips drawn tight. "She's starting to stink."

She's right.

I followed her down the stairs. The boards creaked beneath my weight. The smell wafted toward me, sick and sweet. Though I'd smelled worse, I couldn't stop the reflexive scrunch of my nose. My plaything was dead, laid out on the cement with a dark veil of dried blood around her head. The bright red of the fresh blood was a distant memory. I could hardly recall its texture as it oozed onto the ground.

We shouldn't have left her down here this long. My hand grazed her decaying skin. Memories replayed in my head of when she was full of life—captive, but alive. I shivered. *From sadness or excitement?* Only a few days prior, she'd been beneath me, too weak to fight me off. *It's not as much fun when they don't fight.* I wanted them to claw at me and push me away. *Try* to push me away.

My fingers traced the skin of her neck. I pushed the collar of her shirt down, exposing her bare shoulder. My hand lined up with a bruise on her skin. A bruise that would never heal. *I feel bad, but I should feel worse. I don't want to cause so much damage to them. I can't help that I'm stronger. Besides, they're mine to use.*

"Are you going to fuck her again or help me get rid of her?" Marcy grabbed the woman's legs and lifted them with a grunt.

Not my thing. I never slept with them once they were dead. I liked the warmth of their flesh as they struggled under my weight.

I grabbed the girl's wrists while Marcy wrestled with her ankles. The back of her head thudded against every step as we dragged her corpse up the stairs. Reaching the first floor, we waddled toward the back door. Marcy dropped the girl's legs, and they hit the ground with a thud. She pulled a tarnished key from her pocket and unlocked the deadbolt from the inside. I swallowed hard. The locks were a constant reminder of my purpose in this place.

With my back facing the outside world, I dragged the girl over the threshold and into the chill of the evening. Guilt gripped my stomach and squeezed. For the first time since we captured her, she finally felt the tickle of grass against her skin, but it was only after she was dead. Her soul haunted me —and this place.

After hauling her dead weight up the stairs, through the house, and over the grass, opening the shed's heavy metal door became a monumental task. I pulled it open while trying to catch my breath. The rusted wheelbarrow waiting just inside the shadows would be her temporary resting place. I slipped my hands under her arms and lifted her into the barrow's bucket. Legs which had once kicked at me lay still over the sides.

Stepping back into the night air, a glint of moonlight caught my eye, reflecting off the gun tucked in Marcy's waistband. *She'll never trust me, even though I've never given her a reason not to. I've done all she's asked. Became all she wanted.*

THE STREETLIGHTS PASSED OVERHEAD, occasionally illuminating the snug backseat of the sedan. I watched the lights zip past from my position in the rear floorboard. Marcy sang along with the country music blaring from the speakers. She was tone deaf as hell, and she made up the lyrics half the time, but it never seemed to bother her. I hated that genre, but I wouldn't complain. It was a treat to get out of the house.

"What about her?" Marcy asked.

I poked my head up—just enough to peek over the dashboard and see through the dirty windshield. A woman jogged down the quiet neighborhood sidewalk. She wasn't my type. Her dark brunette hair swished in a ponytail as she ran. She reminded me of other women long gone from this earth. Her strong calves flexed with each step—an unnecessary challenge if she kicked beneath me.

"There's too many lights here," I said with a shake of my head.

"Well, we don't have all night."

"Fine. Turn down that street." I gestured toward a dimly lit road.

Marcy made the turn. We were still in a suburban area,

but the lights were more sporadic, lending darkness to hide beneath. Marcy slowed the car to a crawl as she drove along the empty street. A raindrop hit the windshield. Then another. They splattered and rolled down the glass.

"Rain? Perfect," Marcy said. "Oh, what about her?"

I looked again. A petite blonde walked along the sidewalk, too preoccupied with her phone to notice us. Her loose ponytail trailed over one shoulder, and the curves beneath her tiny jean shorts held my gaze. Her legs were long. Beautifully long. My mouth watered, and my cock stiffened.

"Yes, her," I said with a smile.

"Don't fuck this one to death, okay?" Marcy shook her head.

The last girl hadn't been able to stomach us. She'd chosen to starve herself rather than remain a captive, and I didn't blame her. Her existence centered on being a source of pleasure. Nothing more. That would weigh on anyone, but especially someone as spirited as she had been.

I wondered what could have become of me if she lived. If the dynamics could have changed. What if she grew to like sleeping with me, and I ended up hating her for it? If a rapist's cock could make her come, would that disgust me? After all, it was the fear in their eyes which intoxicated me. The power of inflicting pain and being capable of so much evil. I put the fear of the devil inside them, and it was euphoric.

Even if I cared for my last pet, I wouldn't have been able to stop. Couldn't have stopped.

I eyed the girl on the sidewalk once more and sank back to the floorboard, hiding from the approaching headlights. "Yes, she's perfect."

MACKENZIE

A DROP of rain splattered on the ground in front of me. I looked at the sky, hoping the clouds would hold their contents until I could get where I was going. *That's all I need.* Fat droplets landed on my shoulders and dripped down my arms. They picked up speed, falling in a curtain illuminated by oncoming headlights. Wind pushed against the growing puddles in the street and guided miniature waves across the asphalt. Mother Nature's response to my silent wish. I shivered as my saturated ponytail directed rivulets down the front of my shirt, sending goosebumps racing along my exposed skin.

The houses blurred together. No matter which way I looked, they all had the same features: big windows and long driveways. Mailboxes lined the road, their numbers nailed to the posts. I picked up my pace to get to the next one.

"Shit," I mumbled. The numbers were descending when I needed them to be ascending. The address I was looking for was also odd, not even. Double wrong.

Headlights blinded me as they turned the corner. I started to jog across the street, wanting to walk along the other side. The right side. The speeding car came to a screeching halt, filling the air with the scent of scorched rubber. I apologized with a wave of my hand, and the car sped off as my foot touched down on the opposite sidewalk.

Leaves crackled and swayed overhead. The trees creaked as their trunks moved with the wind. I clutched my purse to my side. *Enough of this.* I dialed my friend's number and put the phone to my ear. Voicemail.

"Allie! It's Mackenzie. I used a rideshare app and got dropped off down the road. I'm in front of house number . . . 1936, and it's really dark here. I'm going toward the 1990s. If you get this soon, please come get me!"

Fuck. Maybe I should call for another ride. My laziness urged me to do just that—and it *was* tempting—but I kept walking. The streetlights were far apart on this street, and as the darkness built between them, so did the knot in my stomach. My mind played tricks on me in the shadowy places. Footsteps thudded behind me, but each time I swiveled my body, there was only dark concrete and empty space. I shivered.

The bright lights of an oncoming car blinded me, and my eyes clenched shut. It turned around in a driveway behind me and followed me at a crawl. I kept my eyes forward, hoping if I didn't acknowledge the driver, they would move along and leave me to find my destination in peace. No such luck. The window lowered with a mechanical whir and revealed the shadow of a woman behind the wheel.

"Do you need a ride?" she asked, the rain pelting her through the open window. Her voice was warm and soft, lulling me into a sense of security.

"No thank you!" I had to raise my voice to be heard over the rain as it pattered against the sedan's metal body. I crossed my arms over my chest, fighting to retain some warmth and stop shivering. *Fuck, it's cold.*

I knew the rules about strangers. Even at thirty, the warnings nagged at my mind. Men in white vans with puppies and candy. But this was a woman. I leaned down to get a better look in the car.

Long, dark hair framed her pudgy face. She flashed a warm, motherly smile. A slight gap separated her front teeth, and tiny wrinkles formed at the corners of her green eyes. She looked to be in her forties. Her fingers wrapped around a Styrofoam coffee cup, tempting me in with a warm drink instead of candy.

"It's freezing cold, and it's raining. How far are you trying to go?" she asked.

"Just down the road. A few blocks, maybe." I gestured,

squinting against the raindrops as they slapped against my face.

"Let me take you. I promise I don't bite." She chuckled.

Warning bells rang in my head, but the heavy rain and dropping temperatures drowned them out. I walked to the passenger side and climbed in. As the warmth inside the car embraced me, my shivering slowed.

"I'm Marcy." She held her hand toward me.

"I'm Mackenzie," I said above the chattering of my teeth. I eyed her hand for a moment, shook it, then pulled away and tucked my arms against my body.

"Have some of this coffee. I got it for my husband, but you clearly need it more." She lifted a cup and handed it to me.

I took it, wrapping my hands around the warm Styrofoam. The liquid sloshed as I brought it to my mouth with trembling hands and took a hearty sip. Heat slid down my throat and filled me.

"What are you doing out here, anyway?" Marcy asked as the car continued idling along the curb.

"I was going to visit my friend for her birthday. We planned on drinking, so I didn't want to drive myself, but the driver dropped me off at the wrong address."

Marcy made a noise from deep within her throat, almost as if she were fighting back a laugh. I took another sip of the heavenly drink and relaxed into the seat.

"What's the house number?" Marcy asked while scanning the mailboxes.

"I'm trying to get to 1998."

Marcy put the car in drive, pulled into a driveway, and started toward the direction I'd been heading. Another wave of warmth washed over me, like a pulse that started in my feet and rose into my brain. It hadn't come from the heater or the hot drink in my hand. It came from within. My eyelids became lead curtains with the next pulse.

"Mackenzie?" Marcy whispered. Her voice sounded far away and distorted.

I fought against the feeling, using every ounce of strength to keep my eyes open. Through the window, the white post labeled 1998 drifted by. I tried to lift my arm to gesture toward it—to tell her she'd missed my stop—but my limbs had become heavy, immovable things. Words lived in my throat, refusing to come out. I closed my eyes and drifted off to the sound of country music and the low hum of the car's engine.

I STIRRED AWAKE. The room spun around me, twisting my stomach with its rotation. I felt as if I'd just woken up from an all-night tequila bender. *Worse than that.* Pain pulsed between my eyes. Water dripped from a leaky pipe above me, every few drops splashing against my skin. The sound nearly kept time with the pounding in my head. The gritty concrete rubbed my legs raw, and my shorts did little to protect me from the bite of the porous floor.

Across the room, a single candle flickered and danced. Though the light was weak, it was enough to force me to squint my eyes. I tried to lift my right hand to cradle my aching skull, but something weighed it down. My eyes adjusted to the darkness as they trailed toward my wrist. I pulled my hand closer to my face, unable to process what I was seeing.

A thick manacle wound around my wrist, attached to an industrial length of chain. The links dragged along the concrete, clanking and scraping against the floor. The sound of captivity. I followed the chain until it ended at a metal plate bolted into the wall.

Adrenaline coursed through me, igniting my body and dulling the pain in my head. My eyes flew around the room as I tried to make sense of my situation. The candle's flame did little to assist me as it danced at the tip of the wick, blissfully unaware of my captivity. A small window peered back at me from the far wall. I couldn't tell if it was day or night outside. The sun and moon would be no match for the mud which coated the glass. Rusty nails jutted out of the sill, nailing it shut. Even though I was slender, it wasn't large enough to escape from, nails or not.

I ran my hand along the cool concrete wall behind me. Even the paint wished to distance itself from this house of nightmares. It flaked beneath my gentle touch, landing on the floor. Another chain snaked from a metal plate on the wall opposite me. Stretching my legs and straining my arm, I could almost reach its tail. Aside from a table and some boxes I'd never be able to reach, the rest of the basement was bare.

I turned back to the metal plate securing me in place. My eyes met dark handprints on the wall. *I hope that's not what I think it is.* I gripped the cold metal chain in my hands and yanked, throwing my full weight backward. It didn't budge. I tried pulling at the edges of the plate, hoping the aging concrete would give way. I snatched and clawed until my fingers bled. It was pointless. The bolts sank deep within the wall, and aged or not, I couldn't move them. Despair washed over me.

My thoughts drifted to my parents. I was a terrible daughter who didn't call or text as often as I should have. They wouldn't realize I was missing until I'd been gone for days. They'd think I was busy or hard at work, not locked up in a goddamn basement. I wanted to believe my friend would call the police, but I was a flighty friend at best. When I didn't show up, she probably assumed I bailed like I always did.

Ways I could be murdered played through my head. Would they choke me? Cut me into tiny little pieces and stuff me in a suitcase? *Oh god.* I tried to swallow, but my mouth had gone so dry, it felt as if I were gulping down sand.

"Help!" I screamed as I looked toward the wooden beams above my head. "Where am I?" My words came out strained, choked with panic. Guttural screams exploded from my throat, shaking the candle's flame with their veracity.

What the hell am I doing? The only person who will hear me is the one who put me down here. I'm calling the monster to me.

Chapter Two

BENJAMIN

Screams. Primal shouts swirled around me like a tornado. *Fuck.* I glanced up the stairs as I threw my magazine onto the couch. If Marcy didn't hear the screams, she most definitely heard my frenzied footsteps as I ran to the basement.

I unlocked the door, and when I slammed it closed behind me, she quieted. I walked toward her and wrapped my hand around her mouth. Her nostrils flared wildly as she clawed at my arms. Her nails sank into my skin, sending a shiver coursing through me.

"You have to be quiet!" I said through clenched teeth. She was small but mighty as she flailed against my body. "If you think I'm bad, *she's* much worse." I gestured above us. "So if you don't want to draw her attention, I suggest you shut the fuck up."

I held her face close to me until she stopped flailing and screaming against my hand. I softened my grip and eased my hand away, ready to wrap it around her mouth again. Sweat gathered on my forehead, and I wiped a hand through my hair. It was longer than hers. I hadn't realized how much it had grown. Unlike my hair, the constant itch and tickle of my beard was a frequent reminder. It made me look older than I was, but it was hard to get access to a razor or shaver. Near impossible.

The girl looked at me the way a snared animal looks at the approaching hunter. She ran her pink tongue over raw and chapped lips. The drug always made their mouths dry. I reached out and touched her face. She flinched, pulling her head away from my hand. The fresh fear in her eyes made me stiff again. To her, I was a monster. *I am a monster. I'd fuck her right now if I could. Fuck the fear out of her face.* I groaned.

Her eyes roamed over my scar-covered arms. So many marks. So much history etched into my flesh. My cheeks flushed as I snatched my sleeves down. My past wasn't her business. The only things she needed to concern herself with were staying alive and being my plaything.

"Where am I?" she asked. The dumbest fucking question they always asked.

Just as I opened my mouth to speak, the door at the top of the stairs swung open. I didn't have to tell her she was in the place she'd die—the belly of the house, where I would rip away, tear apart, and eviscerate everything she ever valued about herself. I would devour her fear like a predator until only her bones remained.

I took a step away from her, putting distance between us. I wasn't supposed to touch without Marcy's permission. She was the gatekeeper.

But there are ways around that, I thought with an uncomfortable throb in my jeans.

"How do you like the new toy?" Marcy asked as she came down the stairs. She held her chin high—the proud mistress of this house of horrors. Coming behind me, she snaked a hand around my waist.

I examined the girl as if she were an object, assessing her value and determining if she was worth the purchase price. Her full lips quivered underneath my scrutiny. My gaze slid downward, hovering over the mounds of her breasts and dropping to the gap between her thighs.

She's perfect.

I didn't dare hide how hard she made me. Marcy hated when I hid it from her. She loved seeing the ravenous hunger of the beast within me. I had to ignore the gnashing jaws and whip him back into the shadows. For now, at least.

"Why?" the girl asked. Her voice quivered along with her chin.

Her eyes kept darting to the light socket above our heads. Burned out wires snaked from the dangling receptacle. Aside from the candles, there were no other light sources. Marcy's little touch. She said it fucked with their heads.

Marcy choked out a laugh as she placed another candle on the table. "Why? What kind of question is that?" She flicked the lighter and ignited the wick.

"Why'd you take me?"

Marcy took slow steps toward her. "You're a replacement for our last toy. We broke that one too soon." She pushed out her bottom lip in a faux pout.

The previous girl had been fierce and intelligent. She was a challenge, always making me plan my actions more deliberately. If she were given even a foot of chain, she'd wrap your neck with it. I'd been disappointed when she died, but I wasn't sure how Marcy felt. She always seemed indifferent when they reached the end.

The girl struggled to inhale a deep breath, choking on the musty basement air. "What're you going to do to me?"

Marcy's eyes fixated as she spun to face her. Under the

shadows of the candles, her features looked mean and twisted. Who was I kidding? She *was* mean and twisted.

"Everything. We're going to do everything to you." She said these words as if she were foretelling of a wonderful gift. In reality, it was a threat veiled in fake pleasantry.

Marcy wiped her hands on her slacks and tugged at the sleeve of my shirt. I sensed her excitement. I knew what she wanted. She wanted me to have sex with her. My stomach tightened with joy at the thought of releasing the ache in my balls inside of this girl. I looked back at her. She'd sunk down the wall and sat on the ground. Her wide eyes stared into the dark as she pulled her knees to her chest.

Marcy squeezed my ass and started for the stairs.

"I'll be right up," I called to her as she left the basement.

I walked over to the girl and squatted down. She flashed sad blue eyes at me, and it took me off guard for a moment. Only for a moment.

"What's your name?" I asked.

Her lips trembled, and it made me throb. "Mackenzie . . . my name's Mackenzie." She wiped tears off her cheeks and dropped her eyes.

I grabbed her chin and snatched her face forward, forcing her to look at me. "Good girl."

She sat up on her knees and leaned into my grasp. "Please let me go. You don't have to do this."

If only she knew.

I pulled my hand away and shook my head. She aimed her desperate pleas at my heart, but they bypassed that part of me and went straight to my dick. Verbal pornography. I left her alone in the frigid basement while I went to feed a snack to the monster inside me. Marcy would be enough for now—an appetizer before the feast.

I CREPT along the hardwood floors the next morning, trying to cushion every step. I'd spent a sleepless night thinking about the things I planned to do to the girl in the basement. Mackenzie. She had one of those rich girl names. The kind of girls that would turn their noses up at me if they saw me on the street. The only thing Mackenzie would turn up at me would be her ass when I forced her on the bed and ripped those tiny shorts from her legs.

The cold metal locks clicked as I slid their bolts away. I opened the basement door and looked down at the plate in my hand—a dry and unappetizing breakfast. A lighter rattled in my pocket as I made my way down the stairs. I grabbed it, flicked it, and lit each candle on the table. The wicks screamed against the flames. I walked over to Mackenzie and squatted in front of her before falling backward onto my ass. I crossed my legs beneath me and put the lighter on the ground beside me.

I slid the plate of food toward her. She stared up at me, eyes wide. Her hands trembled as she reached out and grabbed the plate, nestling it into her lap. She picked up a sausage link and examined it between her thumb and index finger. Her lips curled in disgust, and I was sure she'd put it down and refuse to eat.

I can't deal with that again. I'll shove it down her throat if I have to. It wasn't the only thing I thought about putting in her mouth.

Even if she didn't like what I'd offered, her stomach begged for it with a loud gurgle. Just as I was about to command her, she placed it in her mouth, chewed, and swallowed.

Good girl.

"Do you have to watch me eat?" she asked as she chewed another bite. Her voice was so small.

"Yes, I do. The last girl starved herself, which was pretty much how she died," I said. Memories of the girl in the backyard flooded me. The girl who starved herself to avoid lying with me again.

"Pretty much?" she asked as she shoveled scrambled eggs into her mouth.

I didn't respond. What was I supposed to tell her? It wasn't a game of twenty questions. I had no interest in getting to know her aside from what it felt like to be inside her as she bucked and squirmed beneath me. And I sure as shit didn't want her to know anything about me.

Her eyes remained locked on mine as she swallowed. I watched her mouth, imagining her lips on me. I didn't think of forcing my cock down her throat, which was odd. Instead, I envisioned her accepting me on her tongue and looking up at me with her blue eyes. *A girl like her never would.*

"Are you going to kill me?" She dropped her gaze and poked the eggs around her plate as the words left her lips.

She asks too many fucking questions. "I'd prefer not to." My lips tightened.

I never did the killing. I caused them plenty of pain, and I took treasured pieces from them, but I couldn't kill them. I carried those stolen pieces with me, unable to hide from the ghosts who felt so much anguish because of me. I never wanted to hurt women before Marcy, but now I couldn't look at one of our captives without wanting to tear off their clothes with my teeth.

Footsteps thudded overhead, sending bits of dust and dirt scattering from the rafters. I scrambled to my feet and grabbed the plate off the floor. Marcy wouldn't like me getting too friendly with our new pet.

She appeared in the doorway, carrying a five-gallon

bucket. She walked over and placed it next to Mackenzie. Leaning down, she pinched Mackenzie's cheeks as if she were a child. "How are you kids getting along?"

"I just brought her food," I said, puffing out my chest and standing taller. Her good little soldier. When I was alone, I could almost remember what I was like before all this. Before she molded me into someone I no longer recognized.

"I need to use the bathroom," Mackenzie whispered as heat spread across her chest.

Despite her desire for modesty, I couldn't bring myself to turn away. Instead, I crossed my arms over my chest and watched her. With the side of her foot, Marcy kicked the bucket closer to her.

In the weak candlelight, Marcy looked gruff, her eyes turning downward in the shadows. When placed beside Mackenzie, she looked old and tired. A barrette held her stringy hair away from her round face. When she leaned over to adjust the handle of the bucket, her stomach extended slightly past the angle of her breasts. Even so, I still found beauty in those angles. She was like a mother to me.

Mackenzie stood and started unbuttoning her shorts. The whites of her eyes showed as she stared at me. Even as she lowered the jean fabric down her pale thighs, I refused to look away. Marcy's gaze was also locked on Mackenzie. A smile stretched across her face as the girl's discomfort fed and filled her. I watched because I found her sexy, but Marcy watched for a whole different set of reasons, each darker than the last.

Marcy shifted her weight as her smile widened and became more grotesque. I turned my attention back to Mackenzie, to see what had excited Marcy. A single tear fell from her eye and rolled down her face. Marcy loved it when they cried. She got off on their tears. I liked when they begged, but not when they cried. I could still get off as tears poured from their eyes, but I came a lot harder when they were angry rather than sad.

Mackenzie's cheeks flushed as she buttoned her shorts and looked away.

Marcy stepped forward and stroked Mackenzie's jaw with a curled finger. "You're beautiful." I knew that tone—a deceptive sweetness harboring hatred within its depths. A compliment blanketed by jealousy. Marcy pursed her thin lips as she leaned forward, her mouth hovering by Mackenzie's. "Do you want to take a shower?"

I could hear the deceit in her words, but Mackenzie was oblivious to it as she nodded.

Marcy pulled a keyring from the pocket of her jeans and twisted one of the keys into the lock by the wall. She fumbled with the chain, cursing under her breath as she struggled to release it. Once the chain fell from its base, she kept the tail in her hand and pushed the girl toward the door. Marcy's hips swayed with every uneven step.

Mackenzie peered around as she climbed the stairs. When we entered the first floor, her head jerked in every direction, taking in the new surroundings and improved lighting. Marcy's willingness to show her the rest of the house surprised me. The more Mackenzie saw, the less likely she was to get out alive. But her odds were never great to begin with.

Chapter Three

MACKENZIE

The beast followed behind me. She kept so close that I wore her hot breath across my shoulders like a sour shawl. My eyes darted around the narrow hallway. Yellowing wallpaper peeled away from the wall. Years of thick grime covered the wooden floorboards, creating a tearing sound with every sticky footfall. My arm jerked as Marcy dragged me toward a small bathroom. I looked back at the man. He watched me as the woman leaned over the tub and turned on the water. The chain clanked and dragged against the chipped edge of the yellow ceramic tub. She huffed as she dropped my chain.

"Can I have some privacy?" Even though I already knew the answer, I still asked.

"I want to watch you undress." Marcy's lips parted in a sinister grin, showcasing the slightly gapped smile that lulled me into a false sense of security on the street. "Strip like a good little girl, and I might consider letting you wash yourself alone."

Heat flooded my cheeks. *I'm humiliated.* I removed my shorts and let them fall to the ground. I tried to remove my shirt, but it tangled around the chain. With trembling fingers, I fought to free the fabric. I could feel the man's eyes on me, roving over my nearly naked body. I dropped my panties and covered myself with my hand. I longed to hang on to some shred of dignity. My eyes caught the bulge in the front of the man's pants. It strained against his jeans. I skirted my gaze away, afraid if I looked too long, he'd take it as a sign of interest.

Gross.

Marcy picked up my clothes and lifted them to her nose, inhaling deeply. She ravaged me with her eyes in the same way the man did. She plucked the panties from the wad and held them in front of his face. He took them in his hands, closed his eyes, and buried his nose in the crotch. His tongue slipped from his mouth, seeking out the remnants of what waited between my legs. Breakfast threatened to climb up my throat.

The corners of Marcy's mouth turned upward, but her eyebrows furrowed immediately after—a strange combination of excitement and hatred. The man groaned again as Marcy ushered him out, closing the door behind them.

I held my breath and waited until their voices faded away. My heartbeat crashed in my ears like a string of steady waves against my eardrums. *Could I find a weapon in here?* It was worth trying, and it was better than doing nothing.

I inched open a drawer. The aged metal track squealed, and I paused, certain the couple would come through the door at any moment and find me snooping. I clenched my eyes shut and waited. When I didn't hear their footsteps, I pulled it open the rest of the way. Empty. So was the second drawer. The third held an ancient toothbrush, its bristles brown and splayed out. Its handle had been broken off, leaving only the useless head.

Do they brush their teeth with this? Yuck.

I wrapped my hands around the porcelain lid of the toilet tank. When I pulled, it held fast. I squatted to see what kept it in place. Thick yellow crust ran around the edges. It was glued shut. She thought of everything. There was nothing that could be used against them. I sat on the edge of the tub and fought back a scream.

It was only a matter of time before they returned. Giving up on my search for a weapon, I climbed into the shower, closed the moldy curtain, and let the hot water rain down on me. It tried to comfort me, but nothing could soothe the fear coursing through my veins. A cracked bar of soap looked up at me from the corner of the tub. I suppressed a gag as I gripped it, trying not to think of who else its graying surface had touched. I washed, rinsed, and climbed out. I didn't bother to turn off the shower. Water dripped down my body and landed in a puddle on the floor beneath my feet. The peeling linoleum was cold and slick.

I have to get out of here.

I pressed my ear against the door, listening for their voices.

"You want her, don't you?" Marcy said. Her voice was low and seductive.

The man didn't respond. Not that I could hear, at least.

They sounded close, but not as if they were right outside the door. If I had even a foot of space to run, I had a chance to make it to the front door. My trembling fingers wrapped around the cold metal knob. I sucked in a deep breath and stared ahead, unseeing.

It's now or never. I snatched the door open and ran.

Adrenaline fueled my muscles as I raced down the hallway. The water from my feet mixed with the buildup on the wood, creating a slick surface beneath me. My right leg slipped sideways, and I nearly slammed into the wall, but I regained my footing and keep going. I could see the front door. I could *only* see the front door. I was blind to everything aside from glorious escape.

My fingers flew toward the doorknob like a child reaching for the brass ring on a merry-go-round. Before I could turn it, fingers wound through my hair and whipped me backward. I grabbed at the hand.

"Please, let me go! I won't say anything!"

The man grunted as he yanked me toward the basement. I clawed into the skin of his wrist, but it was no use. He dragged me toward the door as if he were dragging a sack of trash. I screamed as loud as I could, hoping someone would hear. Anyone besides these two psychopaths.

I felt weightless for a moment as the man tossed me down the steps. There was a crunching sound beneath one of my ribs as I collided with the last few steps and rolled to the concrete floor. I clutched my side. Every inhale sent a shock of white-hot pain through my chest. I looked up at the man and wondered if I was looking at the devil himself.

"Why?" I sobbed.

The man came down the steps, two at a time. "You shouldn't have done that," he said with a cluck of his tongue.

Marcy followed behind him with a bamboo stick in her hand. She pointed it toward the carpenter's table. "You know what to do," she said to him.

He grabbed a fistful of my hair and forced me to my knees. I wrapped my hands around his steadfast wrist, trying to relieve the tension between his grip and my scalp. He dragged me to the carpenter's table, climbed on top of it, and pinned the upper half of my body against the rough wood. My breasts scraped against the table.

Marcy thwapped the bamboo stick against her hand beside my face. The sound reverberated in my ears, echoing over the heavy roar of my heartbeat. I struggled against the man, but he was immovable. His grip was sure, and the more I fought against him, the harder he became.

"I tried to be nice to you, Mackenzie, and this is how you thank me?" Spit flew from her lips and landed on my cheek.

An eerie silence filled the basement, followed by the bamboo's whistle as it sliced through the air and connected with my weak flesh. My body moved on its own, my back arching with the pressure of intense pain. A scream tore from my throat. Tears streamed down my face, darkening the wood beneath me. The bamboo sliced my back again as Marcy unleashed a never-ending onslaught of anguish and rage.

Warmth trickled down my side, and the coppery scent of blood overrode the smell of my fear. "Please," I begged. "Please stop!"

Marcy met my cries with another swing of her stick. The pain seared through me and broke through my spine. The man pressed his weight against me. Splinters of old wood sank into the soft tissue of my breasts. I strained against him until I couldn't. I melted into the table, ready to give up.

"I think that's enough," the man said. His commanding tone stopped Marcy mid-swing. He released his weight, and I strained to look up at him.

I flinched, anticipating another hit, but Marcy dropped the stick. It rolled away from her.

She panted and narrowed her eyes at the man. "Lock the little bitch up," she said, and turned for the stairs.

When the door closed, the man grabbed my chain and led me back to the wall. He secured the lock without looking at me. I collapsed to the floor, shivering. There was no fabric between my skin and the rough, icy concrete. There was nothing to comfort me. Only a fiery hatred dug into my bones.

A hand touched my bare back, and I flinched.

"Why would you try to run away?" His angry words didn't mesh with his soft touch.

"I had to try," I said through gritted teeth. I didn't turn to face him. The thought of meeting his haunting brown eyes made my stomach roll.

"There's no escaping from here. Do you hear me?"

The silence suffocated me. I had to appeal to the human inside him. Some semblance of humanity had to remain, no matter how depraved he'd become. "What's your name?" I asked.

"It doesn't matter what my name is."

His eyes were on me. I could feel it. His gaze burned through my back. I curled up on myself, ashamed for him to see me naked, but there was no chance for modesty in that place. His hand reached out and slid through the blood on my side. His fingers glided toward my hip. He let out a groan, and I trembled.

"Please don't," I whispered.

He leaned into me, and his warm breath rolled over the skin of my back. "I will have you," he whispered against me. His words were ice. "I've never gone this long without fucking one of you."

He groaned in frustration, as if it took everything in him not to ravage me. He was a hungry animal, desperate to feed on my innocence. All I could think about was how I could avoid being raped.

I held my breath and prayed to no one. *Please leave me alone.*

The sound of moving fabric came from behind me. Skin on skin. I sat up, looked back at him, and scrambled away until I met the wall. The concrete rubbed against the open wounds on my back, but I stayed against it. I couldn't put enough distance between us.

He stared at me as he stroked himself, rubbing in a slow, sensual motion. I tucked my knees up toward my chest, obscuring his view of my breasts. I'd rather him jerk off to me than fuck me, but I still didn't want to make it easy for him. His eyes slipped lower. My new position gave him a better view of what he really wanted to see. I couldn't win. He twisted his hand around himself, hastening his movements as a soft moan left his lips.

"Stroke me," he panted.

I shook my head and wrapped my hands around my knees. I was tempted to part my legs and let him see what he wanted to see—anything to get it over with faster—but I couldn't. If I couldn't win, I wouldn't make his victory easy, either.

He groaned. Every so often, he'd look up the stairs, like a naughty child watching for their mommy. "I'll cut you a deal." He stopped stroking himself, his cock throbbing with excitement.

"I don't want one," I said, dropping my gaze.

"You haven't got much of a choice. Don't be unappreciative. I don't have to give you one at all." He raised an eyebrow. "You'll remain my little virgin for *now* if you stroke me and make me come. I won't fuck your mouth or your pussy." He leaned into me and grabbed my chin, lifting my eyes up to him.

Jerking him off was better than having him force his way inside me, but the thought of my hand willingly touching him sent a wave of panic through my body.

He stood up, gripped my arm, and yanked me to my feet. He turned me around, pinning my body against the wall. The flaky concrete raked against my stomach and sore breasts.

His heat grew behind me—the warm skin of his dangerous cock.

"Please don't," I pleaded as I trembled in front of him.

"You didn't want to take my deal," he said with a growl against my ear. "I would have taken your hand." His fingers crawled down my arm and grabbed my wrist. "But I'll happily take that mouth." He rubbed his thumb across my lower lip. "Or this." He jammed his thigh between my legs and forced them apart.

"Please," I begged. Tears slipped from my clenched eyes.

Footsteps fell overhead, and he tensed behind me. His eyes flew toward the basement door as a frustrated groan escaped his throat.

"There won't be any negotiation next time," he whispered, and snatched up the zipper of his pants.

My innocence was saved by the devil herself.

Chapter Four

MACKENZIE

I wasn't sure how many days passed since I last heard the door open. My piss bucket was nearly full, and I couldn't hold my bladder much longer. Night and day were indiscernible. Moonlight and sunlight failed to find me.

I ran my fingertips along the wounds on my back. Crusty and itchy scabs pulled my skin taut, but the pain was gone. The physical pain, at least. The wounds left on my psyche would remain with me forever. Or however long the word "forever" meant for me.

For a while, everything hurt. And sometimes nothing hurt, which was even scarier. My stomach had stopped growling, too exhausted to beg for sustenance. My dry and cracked lips no longer felt attached to my mouth. When I swallowed, shards of invisible glass scraped against the back of my throat. My body couldn't keep going like this.

The door unlocked, and a rectangle of light illuminated the stairs. I scooted against the wall as a candle bobbed toward me and Marcy materialized from the shadows. My heart sank.

"Here. Don't say I never gave you anything." She tossed my clothes at me.

The smell of detergent filled my nose. I scrambled to my knees and stood on trembling legs—one-part excitement and two-parts malnourishment. Stepping into my underwear, I tried not to think of the man's look of ecstasy when he sniffed them. My shirt was still warm from the dryer, and I clutched it to my chest before putting it on. It reminded me of using the laundromat in college, waiting to pull the piping-hot fabric from the machine before someone stole my shit. Such a mundane memory, yet I would have given anything to transport myself back to that place.

I slipped my shorts over my legs. Though they provided little coverage, they still shielded my skin as a wave of dizziness sent me against the wall. I slid to the ground.

"Don't get too comfortable, because you're coming with me," Marcy said as she placed more candles on the table.

I shielded my eyes from the flickering light. The candles from before had gone out long ago and left me in darkness. I'd become a cave dweller, my pupils unable to adjust.

Marcy stepped toward me, a smile crawling across her face. "Come on. I need help, and he'll have to clean this up down here. It's disgusting." Urine had spilled from the bucket, creating an undeniable stench.

She unlocked the chain and clutched the tail to her chest. I thought about overpowering her—leaping onto her back and wrestling her to the ground. I encouraged my body to react, but my muscles refused. The logical part of my brain wasn't too keen on the idea, either. It would be an unfair fight. Even in my prime, my slender frame wouldn't put a dent in her doughy body. I stood on shaky legs—a newborn calf being led to slaughter.

"Come on, honey," Marcy cooed as she guided me up the stairs. Her warm hand pressed against my back. Coming from anyone else, it would have been a comforting touch. Even Jack the Ripper had more compassion than these psychos.

Marcy pushed me toward the back of the house and through the kitchen. Starvation drew every ounce of energy from me. My mouth watered at the sight of a banana on the counter. Dark splotches marred its yellow skin. It was something I'd have turned down before entering this house. Now, it was all I longed for. When I reached for it, Marcy smacked my hand away.

"Is this what you want?" She lifted the banana and unpeeled it, taking her time as she revealed every inch of the bruised fruit. My stomach groaned as the sweet scent teased my nose. Marcy took a single bite of the banana before tossing it into the trash. "Silly girl, come on."

She unlocked the back door from the inside. I shielded my eyes as I strained to adapt to the foreign light of the sun. How many times had I strolled along the seashore while taking the warmth and glow of the sun for granted? Would I ever feel the gritty touch of sand between my toes again?

"What are we doing?" I asked.

"You'll see," Marcy said with a sickening smile. She pinched my cheek.

I glanced around as she pulled me through the doorway by my chain. Barren fields stretched in every direction. There were no other houses in sight. No neighbors to hear my screams. Weed-ridden grass brushed against my feet as I turned to face the house. The blue siding reminded me of a cloudless summer sky. The same sky I saw in my mind's eye while dreaming of my life before Marcy.

The man stepped out of the house. He worked a pair of heavy gloves over his fingers. The sunshine caught in his dark hair and sent a shimmering gleam down its length. Round muscles moved and rippled against the sleeves of t-shirt.

Marcy snatched my chain, yanking me around to face her again. The rattling metal was an audible reminder of my captivity. She leaned over, picked up a shovel, and forced it into my hands.

"If you so much as *think* of raising that thing higher than those perky tits of yours, you'll be dead before the devil knows you're missing," she said.

Am I digging my own grave?

I kept my eyes on the grass as the man walked past, his jeans swishing with each step. He stopped at the shed behind Marcy and ripped open the rusted metal door. A wall of odor rushed toward us. My throat clenched shut. I'd never smelled anything like it—the unmistakable scent of rot. It was thick, heavy, and somehow saturated the open air.

Marcy disappeared into the shed, lost in the sound of clanking metal and open-mouthed panting. A wheelbarrow appeared from the darkness. Sickening white skin encased the outstretched arm dangling over the edge. My hand shot up to cover my nose in a feeble attempt to protect myself from the pungent, sweet smell. My stomach squeezed and flipped over, acid burning my throat and threatening to erupt from my mouth. I leaned over and vomited on my feet. The yellow-tinged acid scorched the back of my raw throat.

Marcy stepped aside, revealing the body before us in unbroken sunlight. This girl could no longer hide within the shadows.

Her stringy brown hair created a filthy curtain between the handles of the wheelbarrow. The bloated flesh of her thighs bulged through the slits of her ripped black leggings. Prominent hip bones lifted the waistband away from her body. Even beneath the swell of her decaying flesh, each rib lay visible. The state of her body was an anatomical death sentence. A dirty white t-shirt hung from her shoulders, the fabric trying—and failing—to cover the bruises and scars that read her story aloud. It was a story Marcy and the man already knew. They'd written the ending themselves.

The cost of her freedom had been her life.

I stared at the body, knowing the soul had long since left that vessel. No one would choose to remain in that place. *The girl who starved herself.* I shivered despite the heat of the sun on my shoulders.

The girl's eyes were open and fixed in a haunting gaze, and her flesh was beginning to rot. Discoloration marred the softest parts of her body: eyes, nose, and fingers. Her lips pushed together in an unnatural pout. I looked down at the woman's hand, outstretched over the side of the wheelbarrow. The fingertips were cut up, as if she rubbed them raw on the same concrete I rested my head on.

Marcy tipped the wheelbarrow, and the body spilled onto the ground. The heap of legs and arms contorted into an unnatural position. My stomach twisted on itself again, and I covered my mouth to fight back the vomit.

"You need to bury her," Marcy commanded.

"What? No! I can't do that!" It took all my energy to react. To shake my head. To speak.

Marcy wrenched a dark revolver from her waistband and pulled back the hammer. A metallic *click* froze my legs in place as she rushed toward me and lifted the barrel of the gun until it was level with my forehead. I swallowed the building lump at the back of the throat.

"Drag her to that tree and bury her there." Marcy gestured toward a large oak tree across the yard. "If I have to say it again, you'll join her."

I whimpered, dropped the shovel, and reached for the

woman's hands. Marcy released my chain while keeping the gun trained on me.

An empty gravel road stretched into the distance to the right of the property. I contemplated running, but I wouldn't have managed more than a few feet. If my lack of energy didn't finish me off, a bullet would.

I touched the dry, rubbery flesh of the woman's wrists and recoiled, letting her arm flop back to the ground. Marcy grunted her disapproval.

I blew out my breath before reaching down and grabbing the girl's wrists again. As I shuffled backward toward the tree, her hair shifted, revealing a gaping hole in the side of her head. Dried blood caked the frayed edges of the bullet hole. This told me two things: the man hadn't been honest with me about her death, and the gun aimed at me wasn't just an empty threat. I struggled to move faster.

The woman wasn't heavy, but the effort depleted every ounce of strength I had left. I dropped her wrists and leaned over, bracing my palms against my bent knees. Air filled my lungs in wheezing gasps. From a few feet away, the man tossed the shovel at my feet, narrowly missing my naked toes. He looked down at the woman, his lips drawn tight and downward. His deep brown eyes glistened with a hint of sadness and longing. It was the first time he looked human to me.

Does the boogeyman have feelings?

Marcy cleared her throat. I picked up the shovel and started to dig. The earthy smell of fresh dirt raised up, reminding me of camping trips with my family. I pictured my dad, frustrated as he tried to clear the campsite of rocks so he could drive the metal tent pole through the soil. Memories of my family dripped from me in the form of sweat, and burrowed into the deepening gravesite. Instead of being a comforting thought, it killed me to think of my family and what they'd be going through at this point. A parent's worst nightmare. *My* worst nightmare.

I speared the blade into the soft ground beneath me, stepping on it with my bare foot to encourage it to go deeper. Despite the pain, I pressed down harder. Without weight to put behind each push, or strength to allow my arms to do the work, the task felt insurmountable. I'd have had better luck digging a grave with a garden trowel. At least then I would have been able to sit while I worked.

I took my foot off the blade. The arch ached where the metal dug into my flesh. I tossed the dirt aside and repeated this motion over and over until stars swam before my eyes. The ground rushed toward me. Hands encircled my waist as I collapsed, his grip a confusing mixture of firm and gentle. He laid me on a lush cushion of grass and called to Marcy. I didn't lose consciousness, but I played into it. With hazy vision, I stayed still, staring at the disturbed earth beneath the tree.

"She fainted!" he yelled while leaning over me.

"God damn it! I ask her to do an ounce of manual labor, and she can't even handle that."

"She hasn't eaten in three days, Mar," he whispered.

Marcy stomped toward me and shoved the pistol into her waistband. With bared teeth, she lifted the shovel and chucked it at the man. It tumbled end over end until it landed at his feet.

"Finish this," she said. Shaking her head, she turned and went back inside the house. The door slammed behind her. The sound filled the thick summer air.

The man sighed, picked up the shovel, and continued to hollow out the grave. "I don't want to dig another fucking hole." His muscles flexed as he lifted heaps of dirt and dropped them into the growing pile. Every so often, his eyes would dart to me, making sure I remained immobile.

My arms felt as though they were encased in lead, but my body felt numb. Not even hunger signaled me any longer. The man stabbed the head of the shovel into the ground with a final thrust and stood beside the woman's body. He used the back of his forearm to stem the flow of sweat which dripped from his brow. Too exhausted to lift the corpse, he rolled her into her final resting place and pushed the mound of dirt back into the hole.

My eyelids drooped until I couldn't fight them any longer. I lay on the grass and listened to the steady thump of dirt against a dead body. Even with my eyes closed, sunlight danced and played in front of my lids. I doubted I would ever dance and play again. I would meet my end at the hands of—

Lukewarm liquid washed over me. I sat up with a sharp inhale, sucking some of the droplets across my tongue. The taste was salty, strong, and indescribably unpleasant. My piss bucket lay overturned beside me. It was urine. *My* urine.

I spit the liquid onto the ground between screams. Piss trailed down my face and kept finding its way to my horrified lips.

Marcy removed the gun from her waistband and pointed it at me. "Shut your fucking mouth!" she yelled over my screams.

I fell silent. My chest heaved as I looked from Marcy to the man. Standing over the top of the grave, he compressed the soil with his feet as he avoided my gaze. His lips formed a tight, thin line across his face. He appeared as mortified with the pungent aroma of urine as I was. He grabbed the tail end of my chain and yanked me to feet.

Marcy grabbed his arm. "She's not going into my house like that!"

"What do you want me to do, then?" He threw his hands up and raised his eyebrows.

They talked about me as though I wasn't standing right

beside them. Anger radiated from them the way heat spilled from a roaring fire—invisible yet palpable. It wasn't as if I'd pissed myself. Marcy created the problem by dousing me with my own urine, yet she seemed to blame me for the entire ordeal.

"Spray her with the hose and let her use the dish soap over there. I don't care." She made another dramatic exit, escaping my stench by returning inside.

He led me toward the hose and turned on the spigot. The deflated rubber expanded with a sharp hissing sound. I snatched at the nozzle and put it to my mouth, letting the cool water soothe the back of my throat. He yanked it away, turned the water toward me, and let it fall over my head and arms. With a smirk, he grabbed the bottle of dish soap and handed it to me.

"Wash yourself," he said.

I poured the soap into my hands and lathered it over my exposed skin. I released a sigh of relief as the itchy coating of urine drifted away with the suds.

"Not like that. I want to see." He jerked his chin upward. "Lift your shirt and show me."

My lips trembled as goosebumps rose on my skin. I stood in place, hoping he'd change his mind.

The cold water bit at my flesh and assaulted my tired bones. He threw down the hose at his side. With narrowed eyes and lips curled into a snarl, he marched toward me. I snapped my eyes shut and prepared my body for the impending blow. Instead of the thud of flesh connecting with flesh, I heard the high-pitched squeak of the rusty spigot. I opened my eyes in time to see the rush of water become a mere trickle from the end of the hose. I collapsed onto my hands and knees, grabbed the hose, and let the last drops fall into my waiting mouth. My insides screamed as the cold water landed in my stomach.

The man grabbed my chain, lifted me to my feet, and dragged me toward the house.

Marcy stepped in front of him as we approached the doorway. She looked down at me. Her nostrils flared with every breath, her lips drawing into a sadistic grin. "Don't give her any dry clothes. Just put her back in the basement." Hatred consumed her.

He raised his eyebrows, offered a slow nod, and led me toward the basement. Once I was back in my dismal corner, he locked the chain to the wall and slid my emptied bucket toward me. I couldn't stop shivering. Cold drops of water dripped from my hair and traveled down my chest.

"You really pissed her off," he whispered. He squatted down, balancing his arm on his knees.

"I didn't mean to," I said between chattering teeth.

"Hey!" Marcy's shrill voice pierced the silence. "Here. Feed the thing."

He stood and walked toward the stairs. My mouth watered as she slid a plate into his waiting hands. My body screamed for life-giving food while my mind wanted to boycott it entirely. The man leaned down and placed the plate in front of me. My hunger dissipated when I saw the unrecognizable mash of gruel staring back at me. It almost looked like blended meat.

Gross.

Instead of growling in anticipation, my stomach threatened to flip at such an unsavory meal. I sat back and looked away from him.

"Eat," he said as he sat down.

I stared at him with squinted eyes. Instead of meeting my challenge with an equally intense gaze, he dropped his head. I scoffed, pulling him out of his somber moment. His head popped back up, and he grabbed my chin and forced my head back.

"You *have* to eat." He pushed the plate toward me.

My brain and stomach were locked in a battle, but my gnashing insides finally won. *Beggars can't be choosers.* I reached out my hand and brought a fistful of the soupy meat to my mouth. Without breathing through my nose, I pushed the food to the back of my throat in a failed attempt to bypass my taste buds. The gummy warmth of it coated my tongue before slithering down my throat and burying itself in my gut. I took another handful before pushing the plate back toward his feet.

"Bring her up here! Into the bedroom!" Marcy screamed from upstairs. Her shrill tone coupled with the remnants of meat paste clinging to my mouth were enough to make me gag.

The man lifted his eyebrows, staring at her with an intense knowing. My heart quickened its pace as he unlocked my chain. He wiped at his brow. His legs moved to a different rhythm as he pulled me toward the stairs, like a child forcing himself to walk when his legs begged him to run. When I saw where we were heading—when I glimpsed the rickety bed peeking through a partially open door—I knew what was coming.

Chapter Five

BENJAMIN

I dragged her into the bedroom and pushed her onto an old rocking chair. The metal clinked as I attached her chain to the plate behind her. It had been nearly two weeks since we picked her up, and I still hadn't gotten to play with her. Usually by that point, I'd have sunk into her enough times to shift the inner beast's roar to a tolerable growl.

She looked at me with eyes rounded by fear. Afraid to stick up for herself. Such a mousy thing. Instead of yelling and fighting like the others before her, she trembled and stared ahead. She accepted her fate. A side of me wanted to chain her to the bed, legs spread. The other side wanted to hold her innocence in my hand until I was ready to shatter it. Her fear almost made me feel bad for her. *Almost*. I wasn't familiar with the sensation of something so close to sympathy.

"What's going to happen?" she whimpered.

I couldn't respond, because I didn't know. It would be whatever Marcy wanted. If she wanted me to fuck her, I would take her innocence and pound into it until it became unrecognizable.

Her eyes darted to the photos above the bed. Two framed ducks against pale yellow walls. Her eyes shifted again. I followed them and landed on the snow globes. Marcy had a wall of them. Smiling children building a snowman. A miniature train cresting a snowy hill. Two cardinals perched on a slender branch. But most were various species of birds. The dainty characters bore witness to the depravity we created. They watched over the bed, unable to close their unseeing eyes.

I followed her gaze again. The bed. Its creak wasn't from age but from the groans of abused phantoms. Brown stains marked the uncovered surface—we'd stopped using a sheet a long time ago. It sank into a depression in the center, as if even the mattress wanted to get away from what occurred on top of it.

I looked back at Mackenzie. Dark stains saturated the wall behind her. Old blood that had splattered against the wall and spread. No one died in that room. It was where people wished for death, though.

There were only two reasons she'd be brought in there. To fuck her or force her to watch us fuck. Marcy had been so unpredictable as of late. I didn't know which it might be, but I knew I was getting my dick wet no matter what. The crotch of my jeans tightened.

Marcy walked in wearing a lacy gown. Her nipples strained against the fabric at the bottom of her sagging breasts. She'd fashioned her hair into a single braid, which stretched down her back. She placed the gun beside the pillows on the bed. It drew me in, so close to my reach. Marcy grabbed my hands and placed them on her hips instead.

"I know you've wanted this. You've been neglected for too long." She spoke as if she were gifting herself to me.

She climbed onto my lap and kissed me, her tongue cloaked in a shawl of sour breath and hunger. I dropped back as she pressed her hips into me. The cheap mattress crinkled beneath us.

"I want her to watch us fuck. I want her to wish she were me. That it could be her you were inside of." Her voice was low and raspy.

I snaked my hand around her neck and kissed her again. Marcy spread her lips over mine. Her saliva soaked my lips as her tongue sought its partner. I looked past Marcy. Mackenzie had dropped her gaze. Marcy noticed me staring and grabbed her gun, cocking it. Her arm extended toward the girl.

"If you look away again, I'll put a bullet in your head." Her icy words trailed off and became a soft moan.

She pawed at my shirt, and I helped her by lifting it over my head. Her hands raked down my chest, going lower until she found the waist of my jeans. Already hungry for me, Mackenzie's gaze pushed her into desperation. She loved an audience.

My cock twitched when I thought about how it pressed against Mackenzie's body the last time I was alone with her. I closed my eyes and imagined what could have happened.

Heat enveloped me as Marcy wrapped her mouth around me. A groan rose from my throat as I lifted my hips toward her. I gripped her dark braid and opened my eyes again, seeking Mackenzie's face. I imagined her mouth on me instead. The soft curve of her lips. Eyes that rivaled the color of the sky looking up at me. Instead of fighting me off, she would moan as she sucked me. She would reach her fingers down and play with herself as I came on her face.

I looked down at Marcy. She licked up the length of me,

slow and drawn out. Her green eyes danced between me and Mackenzie. I grabbed the back of Marcy's head and forced it down. Her face wasn't the one I wanted to see. I stared at Mackenzie, wishing she could taste me on her tongue. I closed my eyes and envisioned her fingers raking my abdomen. Would it be from pain or pleasure? I shook my head.

I never give a shit about their pleasure . . .

Marcy pulled away, licking her thin lips. She climbed back up my body and bunched the bottom of her gown toward her waist. With a swift motion, she guided me inside her. Her moans seemed forced and faked, as if she were trying too hard. I hated it when she got dramatic while fucking me. She didn't enjoy it. She got off on the eyes watching us. Or the cries from beneath me. The motions between us didn't call for such animated noises.

I flashed my eyes at Mackenzie again and imagined her riding my dick instead. What would those perky breasts feel like against my mouth? My cock twitched. The intensity of my stare as those scenes flashed across my mind unnerved her. She turned her head.

I motioned to Marcy, and she leaned over and grabbed Mackenzie by the chin. She snatched her head so she faced us, forcing her to watch. She ran her fingertips over Mackenzie's lips and pried them apart, cramming them into her mouth. Marcy groaned as she brought them up to her own mouth and licked up her fingers.

After she lapped the taste away, she drew back and slapped Mackenzie with her wet hand. "Don't look away!"

I flipped Marcy onto her back and leaned over her. At that angle, I could catch Mackenzie's gaze. I needed to look at her. It made it easier to imagine her beneath me. I reached out my hand, trailed my fingers along her cheek, and grabbed a fistful of her hair. A soft whimper passed between her lips. I pulsed inside Marcy. Mackenzie tried to fight my grasp as I pulled her into me and kissed her lips. She didn't kiss me back, but it didn't matter. The salty taste of her mouth sent my hips deeper into Marcy. Even the sound of her rattling chains sent come rushing up my cock.

"Finish on her," Marcy said, her chest heaving.

I pulled myself from between Marcy's thighs, my cock still shining with wetness. I stood over Mackenzie, but it wasn't enough to only look at her. I needed to feel her hand on me. It was a more pressing feeling than drawing my next breath. She looked up at me with doe eyes, her lower lip trembling. She dug her nails into the skin of her thighs. I wanted her more than I'd wanted any other girl, but not like that. Not with Marcy's eyes on me. This one was special.

She's either special, or I'm getting weak.

I rubbed the length of me, my hand rushing over skin that was on fire. My movements slowed. My orgasm came and went, and I painted her thighs with it. A sliver of guilt sprang into my chest as a frown crossed her face. I reminded myself why she was here and squashed the feeling.

Marcy stood and pulled her gown over her heavily dimpled thighs. She reached over and touched Mackenzie's cheek, and the girl flinched as if she'd been hit again.

She leaned toward Mackenzie's ear, her breath hot and tainted by the taste of me. "Soon it will be your turn," she whispered.

The prophecy nearly hardened me again. I zipped my jeans and buttoned them. I threw my shirt over my shoulder, sweat dripping down my stomach. The devil flowed through my veins, sending heat to the surface of my skin.

"Put her back in the basement," Marcy said as she left the room.

I leaned over to unlock her chain. She trembled beneath me—a meek little mouse, scared of the predatory cat.

"Thank god," she whispered.

A smirk lifted my lips. "If there was a god, you wouldn't be in hell."

Chapter Six

BENJAMIN

I released a long exhale before opening the basement door and preparing myself for the stench to assault me. Makenzie sat on the floor with her back against the wall, knees tucked to her chest. Body odor wafted around me. The air was thick with the scent of sweat, tears, and dirt. I brushed a hand through my hair as her eyes lifted to look at me. I placed candles on the table and lit them. While Marcy was away, I wanted to bond with my pet. If I could get past the smell, maybe I'd take her sweet little mouth.

I sat with my back against the wall opposite her, the dusty chain stretched out beside me. I rubbed my fingers along the metal. A shiver dragged a sharp nail up my spine.

I didn't look at her as I lifted my hip and pulled out a pack of cigarettes. I tapped the bottom of the pack before wrestling one out and putting it between my lips. Marcy hated when I smoked, so I could only to do it when she was away.

"Shouldn't you be doing that outside?" She dropped her head onto her knees.

"Are you in any position to ask *me* questions?" I scoffed. "Besides, I can't go outside."

Was I being careless? Yeah, a bit. I just couldn't sit alone up there for another moment while the silence tore at my patience.

"Why can't you go outside?" she asked.

I flashed my eyes at her. "What'd I say about questions?" I lit the cigarette. It dangled from my lips. I lifted a hand to my mouth, gripped the filter between my fingers, and took a long drag. The cherry glowed and crackled. It almost looked mythical.

Out of the corner of my eye, I saw her staring at me, nearly drooling. Her chest eased forward as she watched me. She looked at the cigarette the same way I looked at her.

"Can I have one?" she asked.

"Shit's a bad habit." I shook my head as I held the cigarette between my lips and pulled another from the pack.

"Given the circumstances, my lung health is pretty low on my priority list," she said.

I struggled to keep the corners of my mouth from turning up in a smile. So sassy . . . for a mouse. I lit the second cigarette, the lighter sparking before igniting into a flame. I puffed it once before walking closer and offering it to her.

It lingered between us, still smoking. Her eyes stayed on me, as if I might change my mind and bury the hot end into her skin. She finally took it with a trembling hand and lifted it to her mouth. Would she taste me when she sucked on the filter? I hoped so. I took another drag, filling my lungs with smoke. With each exhale, I forgot more and more that I was a monster and she was my meek little mouse.

"Why won't you tell me your name?" she asked.

I squelched the cigarette into the concrete beside me. The

smell of smoke wafted and swirled around us. *Why the hell does she care so much about that? Do I hurt her any less if she knows my name?*

I stared at her, rubbing a hand through my beard and feeling the soft, dark hair beneath my scarred fingers. "Because my name doesn't matter to you. It's never mattered. I'm not asking you to call me a damn thing." My harsh words held their own secrets.

"Well, if I'm going to die here, the least you could do is tell me what your name is."

I lit another cigarette and ignored her. The question circled around my head. *Why is this important to her?* Probably because it gave her something to tell the cops when she escaped. But she wouldn't escape. They never did.

After a few drags, I finally spoke without looking at her. "Call me Benjamin."

"Benjamin." She echoed me with a nod. "How long have I been here?"

"Two weeks and some change."

"Two weeks?" She groaned and dropped her head into her hands.

"Just be grateful I haven't taken you yet." I blew out a heavy breath. *Why do I have to be such a dick? I don't need to threaten her. She's already terrified of me. As she should be.*

When the smell of her trumped the cigarette smoke, I began to breathe through my mouth. She flashed her eyes at me—a ghostly blue color that made me swallow hard.

"I really need a shower, Benjamin." She said my name. Pleading to my humanity.

Don't bother, there's none left.

"Not going to happen." I shook my head and dropped my gaze.

"Why?"

"Remember what happened last time? Cause I remember."

"I smell so bad that I'm nauseating myself," she pleaded as she squelched the cigarette on the concrete. The smoke circled around us.

"If you were mine . . ." I shook my head, unwilling to finish my sentence. I knew who owned her, and it wasn't me. Her comfort wasn't worth the risk of a bullet. Allowing her to shower was out of the question. I looked toward the doorway at the top of the stairs. "Wait here."

"Where else would I wait?" she mumbled under her breath.

Once I turned away from her, I let the smile creep onto my face for a moment. The absurdity of such a small gesture weighed on me, and my expression stiffened again. I walked upstairs, trying to find something she could use to clean up with. I whipped open drawers and cabinets but found nothing of use. An unopened pack of lavender-scented wipes lay buried beneath towels under the bathroom sink. I tucked it beneath my arm and headed back into the basement.

Her eyes lit up, and a pathetic smile spread across her face as I tossed the bag of wipes at her. She pulled at the plastic, trying to get them open. They finally ripped apart. White towelettes spilled onto the dirty concrete.

I leaned back against a wooden beam, watching her. "Just remember this next time I kiss you. I expect a little more from you, mouse."

She scooped them off the floor and scrubbed at her face. Holding the wipe to her nose, she breathed in the calming scent. She went to work on her arms. When the cloths became too brown to use, she dropped them to the floor and reached for a fresh handful of clean ones. Her eyes closed as she wiped beneath her armpits, and a look of ecstasy played across her face. It was as if she forgot I was in the room in her desperate need for cleanliness. She leaned back and unbuttoned her shorts, but stopped, remembering my presence.

"Can you turn around?"

"Not a chance," I said as I leaned harder against the post.

She hesitated for several moments before accepting I wasn't going to take my eyes off of her. I was going to keep watching her. She lowered the wipe down the front of her shorts. Her cheeks flushed as she cleaned herself. The lavender scent overpowered and mixed with the smells of sweat and piss.

My cock hardened against my jeans. She looked so helpless. She needed me.

The distant crunch of tires against pavement drifted through the thin pane of the dirty window. I tensed, trying to hide my fear from her. I scrambled to pick up the discarded wipes and toss them into the bucket. I snatched the last one from her hand. The one she'd rubbed between her legs. Without another word, I carried it all up the stairs.

Marcy came through the door just as I reached the basement door. "Go to the bathroom so I can lock up," she said. "You know you aren't supposed to be out here when I get back." A lying smile sat on her face. She spoke the words as if they were a request.

I knew the truth.

I lifted the bucket and shook it. "I need to empty this first."

Her face screwed up, and she tilted her head to the side. "What's that flowery smell? You didn't let her shower, did you?"

Busted. I hadn't considered how the lavender scent might linger. "Of course not. I grabbed some dried-out wipes and made her clean up. I couldn't take her smell anymore."

She stood silent, considering my words. She released a

sigh and waved me off. "Whatever. Just leave her bucket by the bathroom door and get back to the basement. I'll be right down."

Sweat collected on my brow. I dropped the bucket and returned to the basement, hoping she hadn't noticed. I wiped it away before she reached the bottom of the stairs.

"I don't like how Mackenzie acted during our date last night," Marcy said. "I told her not to look away, and she did it not once, not twice, but *three* times." She turned—a demon cloaked in the skin of a woman—and faced Mackenzie. Her eyes narrowed until they were slits in her face. "Are we too disgusting for you?"

"No," Mackenzie whimpered.

We *did* disgust her. It was obvious. She clearly hadn't been forced to do a damn thing in her life. Everything on her terms. Shit, even her captivity was more on *her* terms than ours. I'd never gone so long without touching one of my pets. I'd also never been so torn. A distinct line divided me in half. Part of me wanted to hurt her—to selfishly rip her apart—and the other half wanted to take care of her. I curled my lip at the latter.

"It's clear we repulse you, and that won't be tolerated here. You better figure out a way to find us attractive because soon you'll be pleasing us both." She drew her hand along her waistband in a seductive gesture.

"I do! I do find you both attractive." Tears slipped down her cheeks as she lied to our faces. Which was fine. I didn't care if she lied.

"You're a disrespectful, lying little cunt." Marcy turned toward me. "Unlock her and bring her over to the table." Marcy barked her orders at me. She was always snapping at me now.

I rolled my eyes.

Growing impatient, she shifted her weight to her other

hip. "Now!"

I unlocked Mackenzie's chain from the wall. Marcy tore it from my hands and pulled it toward her chest as if she had won a prize. Her eyes lit up.

"Wait!" she shouted. Her eyebrows lifted, and her eyes went as wide as her smile. "I have a better idea. Grab the rocking chair from the bedroom! And zip ties!"

I went and got the rocking chair from the upstairs room. One of the rockers bumped against a snow globe on the shelf, knocking it to the ground. Liquid and fake snow puddled at my feet. The little ceramic eagle which stood in the center of the globe had come away from its base. It looked up at me with cold eyes.

An eagle. The symbol for freedom. How fucking ironic.

I kicked the mess under the bed. I'd clean it up later and hope Marcy wouldn't notice. I grabbed a bag of zip ties from the junk drawer in the kitchen and stuck them in my back pocket. With the chair gripped firmly in my hands, I returned to the basement.

"Set it down!" Marcy commanded. Her voice crawled like spiders along the walls. She flashed a sadistic grin at Mackenzie.

I knew what was coming. Pain in an unusual amount, even for Marcy.

Marcy tugged Mackenzie's chain, yanking her body forward. She dragged her to the chair and sat her down with a rough shove. Placing one hand on each arm of the rocker, Marcy lowered her face to Mackenzie's until their lips were an inch apart. I couldn't help but imagine their mouths touching.

"Zip tie her wrists and ankles," Marcy said as she looked over at me. She brushed Mackenzie's hair from her cheek in a tender way.

Mackenzie snapped her eyes shut and turned her head.

Marcy's soft gaze hardened. With a guttural shout, she drew back her palm and slapped it across Mackenzie's face.

"That's the problem!" she shouted. "She won't look! But I've got something for that. I'll make sure she thinks twice before looking away again. She'll beg us to fuck in front of her by the time I'm through."

Before Marcy could strike her again, I pulled the bag out of my pocket and opened it. I shook some ties into my hand and clenched them in a tight fist. When I leaned over Mackenzie, I almost thought I heard her heart thumping against her chest. Her eyes looked up at me, searching for compassion that wasn't there.

The tie made a zipping sound as it tightened on her wrist, her hands hanging over the arm of the chair. She tried to squirm beneath me, kicking out wildly. Her foot caught me in my kneecap.

Fucking bitch.

I almost struck her out of instinct—out of habit—but I let my fist connect with the arm of the chair instead, splintering the wood and scraping my skin. I took a step back and babied my knee.

Marcy cracked Mackenzie across the face with an open hand. The sound electrified the air around us. I shifted my weight off my knee, and with a harsh exhale, I used my body to pin her legs and tie them off. As I zipped up her last free limb, I stared at her with fire in my eyes. I usually loved when they fought me. When they were a little spicy. But not this time.

"This is what I mean! She's unruly!" Marcy pointed her finger and waved it wildly toward the girl. She didn't even try to hide the excitement in her voice.

She turned on her heel and marched to the table. She eyed the lit candles like a woman judging livestock at the county fair. Deciding on the two blue ribbon winners, she took one in each hand and returned to Mackenzie. She sat at her feet and placed one candle to each side of her. The girl's eyes bulged, and her chin trembled as realization washed over her.

Marcy's fingers crawled up Mackenzie's bare thighs, rubbing a rough hand between her legs. Mackenzie thrashed at the unwanted touch.

"Can you not enjoy *any*thing?" Marcy pulled away from her, reaching out and enveloping each of Mackenzie's hands within her own. She squeezed them as if she were saying a farewell.

The flames swayed as Marcy lifted each candle by its base. Her green eyes locked on Mackenzie's, the flicker of fire reflecting in her irises. With a slow draw of breath, she held the candles beneath Mackenzie's hands so she could feel the heat.

"Fire is such an interesting element," she said. "So permanent. Nothing burned ever goes back to how it was."

"Please," Mackenzie begged. "You don't have to do this. I'm sorry!" Her fingers twitched and flexed at the ends of her wiggling wrists.

Marcy's lips tightened, and she shook her head. "Sorry for what?"

"For not watching you. I liked it. I swear!" Tears slipped down her cheeks and cleared a path through the leftover dirt on her face.

Marcy let out a soft laugh through teeth clenched in an unnatural smile. "No you didn't, and now you're lying about it."

The lies just angered Marcy. It was obvious we disgusted her, and she'd have been better off admitting it.

Marcy raised the candles, forcing the heat closer to Mackenzie's hands.

"Yes, yes I did!" Mackenzie's strained and desperate voice echoed off the walls.

"You think we're disgusting!" Marcy snarled. "Who are you to judge us? What we like?" She lifted the candles higher.

The flames licked at Mackenzie's flesh in quick lashes. She flailed against the zip ties, but all it did was tear at the skin of her wrists.

"Hold her back!" Marcy looked up at me.

I walked behind the chair and gripped Mackenzie's shoulders. I inhaled her scent. She smelled like captivity. She smelled like fear. Her screams rose from her throat and assaulted my ears. I could hear her desperate cries in the depths of my mind. She flailed against me, and I grunted as I held her back.

For a mouse, she sure can fight.

I imagined the fight she'd put up if I were on top of her. How hard she'd thrash and strain to get away from my touch.

Tears soaked her shirt. Between each panting breath, spit flew from her mouth and dripped down her chin. Marcy let the flames bite the soft skin of her palms. The room took on the noxious smell of fear, piss, and roasting skin.

"Stuff a rag in her mouth!" Marcy shouted. "I'm sick of hearing her squeal."

I didn't have a rag. I pulled off my sock, balled it up, and shoved it into her mouth. Her muffled screams broke through the obstruction, but it was more tolerable.

Marcy raised the flames against her hands again, allowing them to linger beneath her palms and fingers. Blood stained the clear plastic of the zip ties from the strain Mackenzie placed on her flesh. She bucked and writhed with pain. Satisfied, Marcy blew out the candles, letting darkness wash over us. Mackenzie sucked breath through her nose in short gasps.

Marcy got to her feet, and I backed away from the girl, glad it was over.

Marcy had risen to a new level of fucked up, and I wasn't sure I could follow her.

"Benjamin, sit," Marcy commanded. She rubbed a sweaty hand down the front of my pants. She stroked me until I was hard and my memories rushed with ill thoughts. She gestured toward the girl.

I raised an eyebrow at her, fighting to regain control of my mind. "Don't you think she's had enough?"

"I'm the one who decides when anyone here has had enough. She kicked you! If you let her get away with it, you're weak." She grazed her hand along the frame of her pistol. Her threat hung in the air like smog, suffocating me.

I bent down to pick up the candles, and Marcy cleared her throat behind me. I turned my head in time to see a switchblade skitter across the floor. It bumped against my foot and lay still. I furrowed my eyebrows at her.

She's out of control.

Marcy pushed her foot into the back of my sore knee. My leg buckled, and I fell between Mackenzie's thighs. She tried to clamp her knees shut, but her tied ankles kept her in place. She shook her head at me, pleading with her eyes. Her red, chapped lips moved around the sock.

"Cut her," Marcy commanded.

I wiped sweat off my hands, letting my jeans soak it up. For a moment, my fingers fidgeted and refused to act. My posture stiffened at the sound of the pistol's hammer locking into place.

Nothing is ever a request. I shook my head. *This does absolutely nothing for me. I just like to fuck them.*

"I said to cut her!" She leaned forward and spat the words at me. "If you think I won't blow out your brains just because I sleep with you, you're sadly mistaken!"

I looked up at Mackenzie, the gnaw of guilt ripping through my belly. I sighed and flipped open the blade. Marcy moved the remaining candle from the table to the floor beside me. Shadows broke our features as I ran my hand along Mackenzie's pale thighs. My boner was confused as fuck.

Marcy squatted beside me. The smile had returned to her face. "Go on," she said. "Make me happy."

I took the blade and turned it in my hand. A tiny thought emerged in my mind and grew until my breath became shallow and quick. A vision of sinking the blade in Marcy's throat and pulling until something popped. I forced the thought down. I shoved it back into my gut and buried it. I couldn't do that to Marcy. Not after all she'd done for me.

I clamped my teeth together and set my jaw. My hand raised the blade toward Mackenzie's pale thigh—a robotic motion over which I had no control. She thrashed and shook her head, sending her blonde hair flying around her face. More muffled grunts and cries slipped through the gag. I pressed down, slicing into her, and blood rose to the surface. The dark liquid pooled and dripped between her legs, landing on the wood of the chair. Her bloodshot eyes widened until I thought they'd pop from her skull. Sweat dripped down her face and joined the tears in her shirt.

"Again!" Marcy hissed. She was a child on Christmas morning, and I was Satan Claws, delivering depraved offerings of a blood sacrifice.

I cut into her again. Her abdomen sucked in from pain as her head flopped forward. Spit and snot dripped in a string, and mixed with the blood between her legs.

"One nice thick line for every time she looked away," Marcy said as she kissed my cheek.

I seared into Mackenzie's flesh a final time. A wave of

nausea forced my tongue to the roof of my mouth as the skin parted. Blood dripped onto the floor in fat drops.

I stared at Marcy, my lips tight. The metal clanged as I dropped the knife to the concrete. I felt dirty. I enjoyed the sex, but the torture disgusted me. No one got any joy from this. No one except Marcy.

The air was rank with the smell of burned skin and blood. "I'm done," I managed to say. "All this because she didn't want to watch us fuck? I don't even know who you are anymore! This has never been what we were about!" I motioned toward Mackenzie, who was choking on her saliva and trying to spit out the gag.

Marcy was unrecognizable. More malicious than ever. Why bring a toy in just to torture it? What fun was that?

I empathize too much with the goddamn mouse. I recognize her pain because it's no stranger.

I slammed my fist into the wall. Chunks of old concrete broke off and scattered around my feet. I rubbed my knuckle and shook my head at her.

We were depraved. We had been for the last eleven years. As a younger man, I never knew how far down the rabbit hole Marcy would take me. How I would become the man in front of her, battling with myself over guilt and the desire to be exactly who I was created to be.

The softer I got, the more sadistic Marcy became. She was losing control, and she was trying everything to regain it.

Chapter Seven

MACKENZIE

I passed out in the basement and woke up in frozen hell. I sucked in a breath. My lungs screamed as cold water and ice cubes forced my conscious mind back to the forefront. My breath caught in my throat. I tried to sit up but kept slipping backward. The cold water depleted me of what little strength I had left. Ice cubes clacked against me as Marcy poured another five-gallon bucket of ice over my head.

Benjamin walked in with more bags, refusing to look me in the eye. The ice rose until it covered my hands, which was almost a relief against the burned skin. If only it could numb the painful memories.

With another heave, Marcy poured a final bucket of ice over me, the cubes shaking and tumbling against each other. I trembled so hard beneath the layer of ice, I thought my skin might shake off. My flesh raised in a blanket of goosebumps, and I shivered as my lips went numb.

"Please . . ." My voice cut off, the cold reaching up and squeezing my throat.

I tried again to rise from the pile of ice, but Marcy responded with a quick gesture of her gun. With the barrel pointed at my face, she pulled back the hammer and sat down beside me on the edge of the tub.

"I'll tell you when you can get out."

Benjamin's jaw clenched. The round muscles on either side of his face pulsed. He didn't speak, though I wouldn't have heard him over the chatter of my teeth if he had. The cold bit at my skin like invisible fangs gnawing through my flesh.

"Marcy . . ." Benjamin reached over to touch Marcy's shoulder, but she batted his hand away from her. "Enough. This is enough." He kicked the empty ice bags.

Marcy rose to her feet and locked eyes with Benjamin. He towered over her in stature but not in fierceness. He didn't seem to *want* to hurt people, unlike Marcy. It was so natural for her.

"Only I can say when she's had enough!" she shouted.

"I don't want another dead body on our hands, Marcy. This is stupid!" He lifted his chest, challenging her.

"Stupid? This isn't stupid! It's called discipline." Marcy sneered down at me. "Everyone needs discipline." Her eyes snapped back to him. "Even you."

Benjamin shut his mouth and looked away. He'd challenged her, but she held the trump card. Without another word, he walked out of the bathroom and slammed the door.

Marcy turned back to me, unfazed by their argument. "How you feeling?" she asked with faked compassion as she sat on the side of the tub again. She reached her hand into the ice bath and dug through some of the hard, clear cubes. *"Brr,"* she said with a shiver in her voice. "Mighty cold in there!"

My eyelids drooped. I wanted to close my eyes and sleep.

A blanket of warmth encompassed my frame, comforting me. The shivering stopped. Marcy's mocking words reached into the depths of my mind, but they came through a veil of thick fog. Unable to fight my eyes anymore, I let them close. My slow heartbeat thumped in my ears. I relinquished myself to unconsciousness. A welcome escape.

I WOKE up on the ground in the basement. My eyes raced around. When the chain rattled, it reminded me where I was. That I was still in that nightmare. My clothes were somehow dry.

How long have I been out?

Crude bandages of gauze and tape covered my hands. The memories flooded back. The heat. The cold. All of it. I peeled back the tape, and marbled skin tried to peel with it. I gasped at the sight of my red, inflamed flesh. Despite the pain, I taped my hand again. Even the soft touch of the gauze was enough to send shooting pain up my arms.

The basement door opened, and Benjamin appeared with a plate of food. His shoulders were deflated, as if he could hardly support the weight of his own body. He slid the plate over to me and turned to leave.

I cleared my throat and lifted my hands. "I don't think I can do this," I whispered.

"Figure it out." He waited for a moment, watching to see what I would do. When I didn't move, he let out a groan and drew closer. "Fine."

He sat on the ground and scooted toward me, picking up the fork and scooping some eggs onto the tines. He brought it toward my lips. I opened my mouth and accepted the food like a baby bird. He lifted another bite to my open mouth and stared as my lips wrapped around the metal. Tension built in the front of his jeans. Heat filled my cheeks. His hand wavered, as if being kind to another human being was a new experience.

Benjamin set the plate on the ground and took one of my hands in his. He peeled the gauze back and sucked in a breath.

"I've never seen her do this," he whispered as he touched the damaged skin.

"Yeah, but she wasn't the only one who hurt me." I dropped my gaze to the cuts on my thigh.

Benjamin tightened his lips. "You don't understand."

I understood just fine. They were both fucked up. How dare he act like he cared when *he* was the one who cut me. "You're a monster," I said under my breath.

He recoiled, like he was appalled or shocked by my accusation. He fisted my hair and pulled me into him. "Don't call me that. You don't even *know* the definition of a monster. If you want me to show you, I'll fucking show you. I've never wanted anything more in my life than to have you. To fuck you." He shook his head. "Would a monster be able to resist such an urge?" He stood and paced the length of the basement, taking deep breaths to calm himself down. He tugged at his beard. "If I don't bandage your hands, they're going to get infected." He stopped his pacing and turned back toward me.

"I'll chance it." I shrugged.

"Do you want to end up in a fucking hole in the backyard?" He said it as casual as talking about the weather.

But he had a point. If I was going to go out, it would be on my terms. Not from some shitty infection.

I turned my body toward him and put my hands out with a huff. He reached into his pocket and pulled out antibacterial ointment and clean gauze. He carefully unwrapped my hands, squeezed some of the gel onto my palm, and rubbed it in with a gentleness I didn't expect. His fingers grazed my skin, and for a moment, I forgot he'd forced me against the wall, threatening to take what I'd managed to hold on to so far.

He looked me in the eyes as he grabbed the gauze, wrapped my hand back up, and taped it. His lips pursed with focus as he took care of my other hand. He looked back up at me. A softness hid within his eyes. It was a look close to sympathy.

We startled at the sound of Marcy's voice.

"What are you doing, Benjamin?"

Benjamin bit his lip as he finished wrapping the gauze around my hand. "I'm changing her bandages."

"Why? Did I tell you to do that?" Marcy drew closer and knocked her hip into his shoulder, but he kept a steadfast grip on my hand.

"No, but I don't want her wounds to get infected. It's not the most hygienic situation down here."

She took a step back and pointed up the stairs the way one might command a naughty dog. "Now!" she screamed.

My stomach tightened. He was about to get in trouble for showing me something too close to kindness. His good deed would be punished, and his weakness would be exploited.

His shoulders fell forward again as he rose to his feet and walked up the stairs. Marcy sighed and slammed the door closed behind them. Muffled yelling faded to silence, and I was alone once again.

The worst part about being that lonely was the happiness I felt at the least bit of positive attention, even if it was from the person who caused the pain in the first place.

I watched the shadows dancing on the walls and longed to go back home, or to work, or even to the dentist. To be anywhere but the warped, confusing prison where the villains were turning on each other. I was ripping them apart as they tore me to shreds. They might break me, but I wouldn't leave them unscathed. I was done being their toy. I'd find a way to get out, even if it meant death.

Chapter Eight

MACKENZIE

"Benjamin! Hurry! It's on! Bring her up," Marcy screamed from upstairs.

He sighed and unchained me from the wall. I looked up at him. *Who are you, Benjamin?* I thought as we climbed the stairs. He avoided my gaze and led me toward the living room.

I looked around the awkwardly small room. Gaudy floral wallpaper met wood paneling halfway down the wall. More ducks glared at me from within wooden frames. The mismatched furniture looked older than I was. Floral patterns galore, aged and dingy. A box TV sat in the middle of the floor. The room was frozen in 1990.

Marcy patted the seat beside her on the couch, a broad smile on her face. Benjamin let go of my chain so I could sit beside her. I didn't move. My feet were glued to the floor. When Marcy's lips tightened, he pushed me forward. I sat on the edge of the cushion, keeping as far from her as I could.

Marcy motioned toward the TV. I lifted my eyes and

looked at the screen. Each muscle in my body contracted. I leaned forward, unable to grasp what I saw. A blonde woman begged for information on a disappearance. *My* disappearance.

"My mom," I whispered.

"Doesn't she look absolutely miserable?" Marcy said with a wide grin. Joy simmered and bubbled behind her eyes. "I bet she cries herself to sleep every night." A hoarse laugh erupted from her throat. She got off on the heartbreak.

My mother's makeup ran down her face, painting her cheeks black. Her uncontrollable sobbing made it difficult for her to speak. My father stood stoically beside her, more in control of the pain in his heart. He had always been a stoic man.

My picture flashed on the screen, and the news anchor's voice replaced my mother's. "Mackenzie Reilly was on her way to visit a friend when she went missing. Police found her phone on Solace Drive. If you have any information on her whereabouts, please contact the police department as soon as possible."

A red banner across the bottom of the screen detailed where to report sightings or useful information. I put my hand over my mouth as I fought back tears. I turned to look at Marcy. She looked like she was about to cream herself from the anguish on my face.

"You're a cunt, Marcy!" I yelled.

This wasn't who I was. I wasn't a disrespectful person. But I reached an apex of anger.

Marcy jumped to her feet and filled her fist with my hair. I screeched as she wound her hand in a circle, tightening her grip and pulling my scalp to its limit until I was forced to stand.

"What'd you say to me?" Marcy growled through clenched teeth.

"You are a cunt, Marcy." My voice cracked. Panic overtook the adrenaline when the weight of my words hit me. I'd berated her not once, but twice.

Marcy pushed me back to the ground. The rough hardwood floors tore at my knees. My wrists braced my fall. Searing pain blazed up my forearms upon impact. I glanced at Benjamin, but he cut his eyes, unable—or unwilling—to offer any support. Marcy brought her leg back and kicked me onto my side. I grunted and grabbed my belly. With another quick motion of her leg, she stomped down on my abdomen.

I tried to scream, but it came out as a series of groans. I curled my body to protect my insides. Marcy pulled back her leg and drove her foot into my back. My body uncurled in response as the pain penetrated the nerves of my spine. My hands flew to my back.

Grabbing my hair again, Marcy lifted me to my knees. The raw skin protested against the pressure, but I couldn't adjust my position. I reached toward Marcy's arms. The bandages around my hands made it impossible to grip her wrists. She let go of my hair and snatched at my hands instead. She squeezed and twisted them toward my body. My guttural screams reverberated off the walls.

Oh god, please.

I gritted my teeth and swallowed back another scream, knowing it only excited her further. Pain engulfed my arms. Cutting them off would have hurt less than enduring the squeezing and twisting.

"I'm what now?" Marcy yelled.

I sucked in a breath. *Fuck it. Kill me.* "A cunt." I spoke through teeth clenched with pain, though I knew I'd pay for it later. The words were lava, erupting through the volcano of my lips. They spilled downward, destroying everything in their path. I hoped to be washed into a warm death.

Marcy released my hands and slapped me across the face.

The skin of my cheek burned and swelled on impact. The bite of my words deflected back onto me. Rage twisted her face until I thought she might shoot me where I kneeled. Every feature became tight and angular. Her body trembled with frustration. Now she was the volcano, ready to explode.

The kettle in the kitchen let out a shrill whistle, and Marcy's eyes lit up. She'd heard a secret message in its scream.

"Benjamin, bring me the kettle!" Marcy kept her eyes locked on me as she held her hand toward the kitchen.

Oh god, what now?

His feet remained planted.

"Now!" Her shrill demand rivaled the kettle's cries.

Benjamin left the room, and my heart dropped. I could hear the message now. I'd been here long enough to realize what was about to happen.

I know what's coming. Be strong. I tried to pep talk to myself as Benjamin came back into the room with the old silver kettle. Steam rose from the spout as it whistled with a dying breath. He handed it to Marcy. Her knuckles went white as they wrapped around the black plastic handle.

"Grab her wrists and get her to her feet. I want her hands facing up." Marcy directed Benjamin without taking her eyes off me.

Benjamin pulled me to my feet. My knees buckled, unable to support the weight of what was about to happen. He pressed his body against mine to support me. His arms embraced me, pressing his heat into my back. He grabbed the tops of my wrists and twisted them until my palms faced upward. I tried to pull away from him, but his unwavering grip was too powerful.

"Please," I pleaded. Tears blurred my vision. One slipped down my face as I blinked back the panic.

Marcy swirled her hand in the steam snaking from the

spout. "That's quite hot," she said as she shook her hand. "Did you really think I'd let you get away with disrespecting me in my own house? Did you believe you wouldn't face a punishment for your ungrateful words? I was trying to be nice and let you see your mother one last time, and you repaid me by calling me such a vulgar word."

"I'm sorry!"

"You sure apologize a lot for someone who never seems to learn their lesson. I've got to make sure you don't forget this one." She clacked her fingernails against the side of the kettle, eyebrows raised.

"Are you sure about this, Marcy?" Benjamin asked.

Goosebumps burst along my skin. He'd been breathing against my neck, but as she turned to face him, he held his breath.

She squinted her eyes at him. "Yes, I'm sure. Keep her steady, or you'll get burned too."

His grip tightened on my wrists.

Marcy lifted the kettle, placed the spout above my left hand, and tilted it. The water poured in slow motion, emerging in a thick, steamy stream. It collided with the bandages and sank to my skin. The nerves screamed and sent panicked messages of danger toward my brain. The pain rolled over every inch of my body. Benjamin lost his grip for a moment, and I began to drop to the ground. Water splashed on both our arms.

"God damn it, Marcy!" Benjamin shouted.

I held up my left hand, the bandage now saturated and steaming. My fingertips were almost purple beneath the gauze. The skin pulsed in time with my racing heartbeat. I stared at the damage, unable to comprehend that level of pain. Like watching through a window, seeing a woman I no longer recognized.

"Grab her other hand!" Marcy commanded.

He didn't react at first. He stood to the side of me, his mouth wide open as he processed what was happening. Clearly, this was new to him.

"Now, Benjamin! Or it's going on you instead! This kettle is getting emptied on one of you, so choose!"

He looked down and tugged me to my feet. He wrapped both hands around my right wrist and pushed it forward. I kicked, screamed, and tried to pull backward using my full body weight.

No! The word kept repeating in my head, screaming in defiance, but he was immovable. *Fuck you!* I belted profanities in my mind, unable to utter any words over my screams.

Benjamin turned his head away as Marcy poured from the kettle again. The water still splashed onto his hands and arms, and he cursed under his breath as it hit him. The heat of the water coupled with the candle blisters on my hands were more than I could mentally bear. I couldn't scream over the pain anymore. All I could do was inhale.

When the last drop of water slipped onto my hand, I let out a sigh. I wanted to go back to my spot in the basement. I wanted to sleep. I wanted to disappear into nothingness and stop feeling.

Benjamin released my wrists, and I collapsed onto the floor in a heaving, breathless mess. The water that spilled onto the floor saturated my gown, but I didn't care. It was finally over.

"Sit on her back," Marcy said.

Benjamin hesitated before sitting on me. I squirmed, but it was futile. Marcy leaned down and pulled my gown up to my hips, exposing my ass. I writhed against Benjamin's weight as Marcy touched the hot kettle to my skin.

I screamed as I tried to pull away from the burning metal. "Please!" I yelled.

"Enough," Benjamin mumbled, climbing off me.

I rolled onto my side, leaving my gown raised. The fabric would only irritate the burned skin of my ass cheek. *Fuck modesty.*

With a huff, Marcy walked into the kitchen, fumbled in the closet, and tossed a mop into the living room. I stayed on the floor while Benjamin picked up the mop and started to clean up the water. He nudged me with his foot.

Fuck you!

"Are you okay?" he whispered.

I didn't respond. The relentless pain in my hands and ass made it impossible to breathe, let alone answer him. My skin felt like it was ripping apart beneath the bandages. That didn't even touch on the mental anguish at seeing my parents begging for my safe return. Obviously, I was not okay.

Chapter Nine

BENJAMIN

Marcy pulled me in for a kiss and pressed her dry lips against mine.

It was hard for me to return the affection because my mind was elsewhere. It was on Mackenzie. I hated holding her flailing body while Marcy tortured her. She shouldn't have burned her with the water. But Mackenzie shouldn't have said those words.

Instead of exciting me, Marcy's tortures disgusted me. I had to look away each time Mackenzie screamed. The cries from the other girls resided in my ears for all eternity. They fueled me. Filled my dick with vitalized blood. But Mackenzie's screams made me soft. When I had to hold her or do her harm, I felt something stronger than guilt. A new feeling for me.

The girls rarely grew so brazen during captivity. They came with a certain level of spirit that we worked to break. A starting point we chiseled away until we whittled them down to their lowest point. After ripping down their panties and rubbing my cock against their pussies, they'd check their attitude. Once I finally fucked them, they shattered beneath me. Their personalities oozed from every pore and dripped onto the mattress. By the time I finished, each girl was half the person she was before she stepped into that bedroom. The moment they gave up and surrendered themselves to my assault, I knew I had broken them.

Mackenzie was different. She started complacent and small, as if she were already broken. Instead of finding her breaking point, she found her spice—the thing that made her more like a lion than a mouse. But she was still my mouse. If I'd had my way in the beginning—when I couldn't get my mind off fucking her and burying myself into her until she finally stopped fighting me—this whole situation would have been different. It would have been normal.

I wanted her. I wanted her to the point that my mouth watered when I was around her. Not the way a predator salivated over his next meal, but the way a man in the desert longed for water. To taste it. To savor it. The more time I spent with her, the more she'd wiggled into my head.

My mind was still on her as Marcy dropped to her knees to suck my cock. I imagined Mackenzie's sweet, warm mouth on me instead. Her blue eyes staring up at me, quieting my anger. The boldness in her as she became tougher the more Marcy tried to soften her. I didn't want to fuck her throat as if she were Marcy. I wanted to enjoy it. I wanted every single moment to last so I could feel her soft tongue move along my skin and swirl around me.

That was bad. Those thoughts would get me killed.

With the heat of come in my balls, I pulled Marcy away by her hair. "Can we play later?" I asked.

She looked at me with a moment of suspicion, but she rose to her feet. "I was just doing it for you, anyway." She rolled her eyes, plopped down on the bed, and turned on the TV.

I went downstairs and turned on the box television in the living room. I cranked up the volume to cover my steps. Veil what I planned to do.

If I fucked Mackenzie the way I should have, she wouldn't be this special little girl messing with my head. With my cock still hard at the thought, I unlocked the door and took the basement stairs. She peered up at me as I lit a single candle on the table. I didn't want to see much of her. I couldn't if I wanted to do what I intended.

Before she could speak, I was on her. The predator within overtook me. I grabbed her arm and lifted her to her feet. She struggled and turned her head to face me. Her eyes didn't hold any fear. They glistened with rage. She didn't make a sound as I shoved her against the wall and buried my face in her hair, smelling her scent—which wasn't particularly pleasant, but it was hers.

I opened my jeans with my free hand and rubbed my other hand along the curve of her ass through the fabric of her gown. She was incredible. Perfection in human form. She'd never *let* me have sex with her. If I wanted her—and I did—I had to take it.

Her body heaved as silent sobs overtook her. I ignored her tears, trying to keep my focus on fucking her. Tearing off her clothes and shattering the innocence she held so dearly. Destroying the cocky attitude she got from thinking she had any control in this house. I'd fuck that out of her and make sure she knew she wasn't different from any other girl.

Even though my cock throbbed and ached to plunge into her warmth, I couldn't fucking do it. Even after stopping Marcy before I came, the excitement still ripping through my body like a raging bull, I was torn. My body wanted her more than it wanted my next breath, but her silence nearly broke me.

Weak. I'm fucking weak.

Why had she shaken my entire being, spinning parts of me like a goddamn Rubik's Cube? I'd never be able to get myself back to where I'd been. She made me feel human emotions again. Memories of who I once was. Her torture reminded me of myself, and I felt for her. I wanted to reach out and shield her from the monsters that lurked behind those walls. And it was dangerous. For both of us.

Without the threat of a bullet, raping her was off the fucking table. I'd do whatever I had to if it came to that, but the mighty mouse was safe for another day.

I released her, and she collapsed on the floor, chest heaving. She looked up at me, somehow more mind fucked than if I raped her.

Same, kid. Same.

As soon as the basement door squeaked open, she slid closer to the wall and wrapped her arms around her knees. I was the last person she wanted to see, but the tangy smell of infection hung over her like a cloud. It permeated the small space. Whether she hated me or not—which she most certainly did—I needed to tend to her wounds.

Her hands shifted and balanced palms-up on her knees. She remained voiceless and kept her gaze on anything that wasn't me.

I pulled a roll of bandages from my pocket. "You need to let me help you."

"I don't want anything from you. Especially not help."

I don't know why I wanted to do something for her, but I

did. Like a master harpist, she plucked at what little heartstrings I had left. She played a song I didn't want to hear, but I couldn't ignore it.

I sat on the basement floor in front of her. I touched the scars on my arms and remembered the pain—a nagging, stabbing sensation that washed over me like a wave at high tide. It surrounded and buried me.

"Fuck you," she whispered through clenched teeth.

Fair reaction. I fought back a smirk. This shit was why I continued to spiral down a funhouse slide of feelings. Only it wasn't fun. It was horrifying on this rickety, splintering wooden slide, and I wanted off.

"What do you want from me, mouse?" I knew what she wanted. No fear of assault, sexual or otherwise. Freedom, for sure. But she needed to ask me for something I could actually give her.

"Please kill me," she said with a humorless laugh.

My gaze snapped up the stairs. "If Marcy hears something like that, she won't stop until you're sure you actually wanted to die, and then she'll force you to live."

"What does it matter to you, anyway? You guys would just get someone else."

My gaze fell. It was true. We would. It was hard to find the perfect girl. Willing and pliable. Someone who could conform to what we wanted. After the last girl died, I told Marcy I wanted it to be me and her for a while. I was tired of that life, but it was never about me or what I wanted. The more I thought about it, the more I came around to her way of thinking. I wanted a new plaything. What a circle jerk.

I opened and closed my mouth because I had so much I wished I could say, but the words were trapped on my tongue. "You have no idea."

Her head swiveled toward me. "I think I have a pretty good idea. Let me know if I've been following this correctly.

You guys abduct women together, make them watch you fuck, torture them, and then kill them when you're done with them."

Her words caught me off guard. The gall she had. The truths she laid out in front of me. "No . . . well . . . yes. But it's not what you think. There's more to this than you know."

"Enlighten me." She threw up her hands and winced from the pain.

I hesitated and considered pouring the truth down her throat. I wanted to put that in her throat more than I wanted my cock there. I wanted her to swallow all of it. I never wanted to tell someone my secrets before. To level with one of them, rip apart my insides, and let myself be vulnerable. But I couldn't because it would change everything. The dynamic would shift. I couldn't let a captive come in and destroy the delicate balance. Though, in some ways, she already had.

"I can't," I mumbled.

"Of course you can't." She shook her head and turned away from me.

I reached out and touched her arm. Dry skin met my fingertips. Frustration rose in my throat. *Tell her the truth. Tell her everything*. I shook my head. "I'm *trying* to treat you right."

Her head snapped toward me. Even in the dimly lit room, anger shined in her eyes. "Are you kidding me? You're just as sadistic as Marcy! You've held me down, and you've cut me. *You!* Have you forgotten what happened in the bedroom? Twice against this very wall? Don't you dare say you're trying to treat me right. What kind of fucked up world are you living in that this is considered good treatment?" She strained her words through clenched teeth to keep from raising her voice and rattled the chain on her arm to emphasize her points.

I narrowed my eyes, the frustration spilling over my lips. "I've never gone more than a few days without sleeping with one of you. It has taken *everything* in me not to take you against your will."

"Oh, fuck, how ever can I thank you for your sacrifice?"

Oh, little mouse, what big teeth you've grown. My shoulders fell forward.

I wished I could tell her my story to help her understand why I was the way I was. I had been molded into this. That house held nothing but monsters and the bones of their meals.

"Can I at least bandage your hands?" I said at last, my words breaking the uncomfortable silence.

She put out her arm and offered her hand without looking back at me. I peeled the tape away and removed the gauze. Raw and red skin shined up at me. Some areas had begun to heal, leaving raised lines along her flesh. The scars would always remind her of the abuse. Scars similar to mine.

"Some of this looks like it's infected. Marcy went to the doctor to get antibiotics we can give you. I think that will help."

"I'm not taking anything from her." Mackenzie shook her head and pulled her hand away from me.

"I don't think you understand, mouse. If you don't, and you get sick, she *will* kill you." My stiff words hid softness beneath the surface. As much as I hated keeping her there—despised what she did to everyone in that house—the thought of her death caused more dread than it should have.

The light flickered across her face, drawing shadows into my line of vision. "Is that what happened to the woman under the tree?" she asked.

My gaze dropped. "No, she starved herself." *Half-truth.*

Mackenzie sucked her teeth, shaking her head. "I saw the gunshot wound, Benjamin, so don't lie to me."

"She wouldn't eat. She starved herself until she couldn't even lift her head off this floor. Marcy just put her out of her misery."

Mackenzie's mouth dropped open. "That's really how you see that?"

"She was suff—"

"She was suffering because of *you!* She was killed because of *you!* She wasn't some animal, hit by a car and still breathing. If she was, it was definitely one of you behind the wheel! Neither of you are empathetic angels of death. You guys are rapists and murderers!" Mackenzie's words exploded from her throat, flowing out of her like vomit. She found her voice, and she was going to use it.

"Don't call me that," I whispered.

"What? A rapist? Or a murderer?" Mackenzie curled her lips and shook her head, unable to drop her gaze from mine.

"A murderer." I wasn't a murderer. Not directly, at least. I never killed anyone myself.

"So that's your boundary line? Murder? You're telling me you haven't murdered any of the women you've captured?" Mackenzie scoffed and turned her hands palms-down as her slender arms balanced on her knees.

Silence washed over us.

"Regardless, you're a rapist," she mumbled.

I got lost in memories of holding down women beneath me as they screamed and struggled. The sounds of Marcy's encouraging and flirty words behind me. The barrel of the gun aimed at us both. The fear of being unable to perform and knowing that would be suicide. The will to live was stronger than the dignity I smothered beneath me. I remembered wanting to comfort them when it was over, but they would never accept the kind touch or words of the monster who violated them so intimately. I wouldn't have either.

I fast-forwarded to the memory of the first time I didn't

need to have a pistol to my head to follow Marcy's commands. I embraced the pleasure I began to feel, letting it transform into pain and fear before thrusting it back inside the vessel beneath me. Marcy's excitement reached into my chest and clawed into my ailing heart. My desire to please her became too vital to overlook any longer. Even after everything she did to me, I somehow loved her. Even though she'd tell me she had those feelings for me, Marcy wouldn't lose an ounce of sleep over sending a bullet into the skull of her beloved. She wasn't afraid to punish me or consider me collateral damage to protect herself. If I got myself killed, it would only be my fault for being so weak.

The door slammed upstairs, and Marcy's footsteps clomped on the floor above us. I stood and stepped away from the girl. Her steps drew closer, and she entered the basement with a bottle of pills and a glass of water. She kneeled in front of Mackenzie while twisting open the bottle and poured a white pill onto her hand. With a blank stare, she pushed her hand toward the girl.

"No thank you," Mackenzie whispered, shaking her head.

Marcy scoffed and shifted her weight, popping out her hip. "I had to go to the doctor to get you these. Don't be unappreciative."

"I don't need them," she said with clenched teeth, as if biting through the pain.

"You most definitely do. I can smell the infection." Marcy wrinkled her nose.

When Mackenzie didn't reach out her hand, Marcy reached down and grabbed it herself. She squeezed and dug her fingertips into the raw flesh of her palm. Mackenzie screamed. As she opened her mouth to yell, Marcy dropped the pill into her mouth. She used one hand to pinch Mackenzie's nose shut. With the other, she pressed against her jaw, holding her mouth closed until the girl was forced to swallow.

"There. That wasn't so hard, was it?" She let go and gave Mackenzie's cheek a light pat.

Mackenzie cradled her hand, prioritizing one pain over the other. Tears filled her eyes, and she tilted back her head to keep them from falling.

Marcy stood and brushed the dirt off her pants before turning toward me. "She's the worst. We haven't even gotten to have any fun with her. I mean, I love when they have a little spirit, but I'm getting impatient with this one. If she doesn't start to behave and appreciate what we do for her, I don't think we'll be keeping her."

Won't be keeping her? But at least she'd die whole.

Chapter Ten

MACKENZIE

I looked down at my unbandaged hands. My skin was almost healed. Shallow scars lined my palms and wrapped around my fingers. That's how long I'd been there, however long that was. I managed to mostly keep my composure . . . and my dignity. Neither of my captors made it inside me. Despite how impossible it seemed, I had begun to navigate Marcy a bit more. Though, reading her was as difficult as trying to make sense of a crumpled and torn road map written in a foreign language.

Her moods shifted like sand. I never knew which version of her would come down the stairs each day, and I was grateful for the days she didn't come to the basement at all. I was even more grateful when Benjamin stopped trying to rape me. It had been weeks since he last tried. He seemed to almost pity me.

The food had been worse than ever, and sometimes I received none at all. I'd always heard stories of people eating stale bread in captivity. Lucky them. The bread given to me was always saturated with copper-scented water. Slop.

Marcy made a point of showing me my story in the newspaper. My disappearance went from front page sensation to barely a mention, lost within stories of a new hardware store on Second Avenue and the adoptable pets at the local animal shelter.

The door rattled and opened. Marcy appeared in the doorway, as if summoned by my thoughts. Her nose scrunched as she came closer.

"Wow, you are ripe!" She waved her hand in front of her face.

I didn't need to lift my arms to verify her statement. The odor hung heavy in the air around us, unmistakable. I merely shrugged in acknowledgement.

Marcy walked over, unlocked the chain, and led me upstairs toward the bathroom. With a quick tug, she dragged me into the room. After closing the door, she let the chain fall to the ground. It rubbed against the old tile with a metallic scrape.

"Give me your clothes so I can wash them," Marcy said, wiggling her fingers impatiently toward me.

I slipped my shirt over my head and unbuttoned my shorts. They dropped past my slim thighs. Marcy stared at my naked body with unhealthy admiration. She bit her lip and snatched my clothes away as admiration warped into jealousy.

"I'll be outside the door, so don't do anything stupid," she said with a harsh glare before leaving and slamming the door behind her.

I looked at myself in the rust-speckled mirror. Greasy, matted hair hung from my scalp. Sunken eyes stared back at me. Dark brown coloration circled my lids. My pale lips trembled at the sight of my body. Skin stretched over bone. I could count each rib above my prominent hip bones. I was already trim before getting thrown into a basement to starve in the dark.

Captivity is not a good look for me.

I brought my hands toward my face and shuddered. The skin reminded me of spider webbing or the marbling of a countertop. I knocked away a tear that slipped past my defenses. It wasn't the time for crying. Feeling sorry for myself did me no good.

I turned on the shower and stepped in before it even warmed up, letting the cold water electrify my senses. Little more than a trickle managed to break through the limescale caked within the old showerhead, but it was enough. The pipes rattled behind it. Brown liquid pooled around my skeletal feet as the dirt from my skin washed away and swirled around the drain. I leaned my shoulder against the mold-stained wall and let the water fall down my scarred back. It slid over thin pink and white marks where the bamboo stick bit at my flesh and took pieces of me with it.

Closing my eyes, I imagined myself somewhere else. Stuck in a dingy motel, like that time I went to New England for a work conference. The hot water had been the only good thing about the seedy motel filled with bedbugs and black mold. It was still preferable to where I was.

I picked up the cracked bar of soap and washed my arms, across my chest, down my stomach, and between my legs. Being able to wipe the grime from my most intimate areas almost made me feel human again. I picked up a cheap bottle of shampoo and turned it over, spilling some of its contents onto my hand. I washed my hair and groaned at the feeling of cleanliness on my scalp.

Marcy knocked on the door. "Are you almost done?"

I rinsed in a hurry and turned the water off. The remnants dripped down the curves of my body. I reached out and grabbed a towel, carefully wrapping it around myself. When I stepped out, a lacy gown waited on the counter, neatly folded.

I shook my head. "I'm not wearing this!" I yelled through the door.

"Put the gown on, dear," Marcy commanded in a soft and pleasing tone. It was scarier than her harsh one.

I stared at it for a moment before picking it up. The soft silk played across my fingers, and I put it against my face. With a sigh, I slipped it over my head and pulled the chain through the armhole. I had no choice.

"I'm dressed," I called out.

Marcy opened the door, grabbed the tail of my chain, and jerked me out of the bathroom with unnecessary force. She guided me past the door to the basement, and my heart sank as I realized our destination. I planted my heels against the old hardwood floor. Even stalling for a few seconds was better than just letting it happen. Marcy stopped walking and turned to face me. With a grunt, she yanked the chain toward her, pulling my face inches from hers.

"Stop being this way, Mackenzie!"

"I just want to go back downstairs!" Though I'd spoken them, my words surprised me. *How fucking pathetic.*

"Well, you aren't going downstairs right now." She smiled and gave the chain another jerk as she tugged me into the bedroom.

When I continued fighting, she wrapped her hands around my arms and shoved me onto the mattress. She pinned my arms beneath me with her knees, grabbed my chain, and leaned toward the headboard. I tried to pull away and roll out from under her as she folded the chain around the wood and secured it with a lock. Finished, she stood back and admired her work for a moment before walking out of the room without uttering another word toward me.

I stared at the ceiling. My eyes followed the path of the brown-stained crack that rushed across the room in the shape of a lightning bolt. The bed creaked as I shifted my weight, my gown rising up to expose the bare skin of my hips. I screamed in my head, fear gnawing at me.

This was it. This was when I'd lose the last thing I held dear. He would end up the last man I ever slept with, and the thought made my chest heave.

BENJAMIN

I WALKED into the room that once felt like drugs in my veins. A high like no other. This time, it felt uncomfortable. Almost like a job. I rubbed the front of my pants, trying to wake up my dick. I still wanted her. There was no doubt about that. I fucking dreamed of her.

"Hey! No, no, you don't have to do this," she began to plead.

Her words made me twitch with excitement. As much as I didn't want it this way, her cries were otherworldly. They went right through my ears and pumped blood into my cock. There was something about a beautiful girl begging for you to stop.

"Yes I do," I whispered.

Even if I didn't want to do it, I had to. She could beg all she wanted, but it wouldn't change the course of what was to come. Her time was up. She was lucky she'd maintained her innocence for as long as she had. Marcy said it was now or never. If I couldn't fuck her, she would be "put down." Marcy was sick of feeding and caring for her when neither of us got anything from her. Frankly, I was sick of watching Marcy come up with torture methods and listening to her rant about how much she hated my little mouse. Part of me wondered if she'd be better off if I refused to fuck her—to let Marcy do what she wanted all along. The other part of me wanted to sink so deep inside her that I could feel the pulse of her panicked heartbeat.

That part won.

"I'm not going to hurt you, mouse," I told her. It wasn't reassuring, but I had no intention of causing her pain the way I had with others. I tried to comfort her. "I'm just going to use you. I'll be quick."

"Please," she said.

Marcy pushed past me. "Oh, isn't this a pleasant sight," she cooed. She ran her hand between Mackenzie's breasts and down toward her hips. She tented the fabric of the gown and slipped her fingers inside. "She's so tight."

Mackenzie cried out.

Marcy's words excited me because it was what I expected. What I hoped for. The aching throb in my cock pulsed within my jeans, even as my mind fought against my hunger.

Marcy pulled out her fingers and licked them. "Taste her," she said, turning to me.

I welcomed her fingers into my mouth.

Marcy tugged me closer to Mackenzie. "Rub him," she commanded.

Mackenzie shook her head furiously, tears sliding past the creases of her eyes.

"I said rub his fucking cock!"

When Mackenzie didn't move, Marcy grabbed her hand and put it against me. Her skin was so warm that I could feel it through the fabric.

"Take your pants off," Marcy said as she looked at me.

I unbuttoned my jeans, unzipped them, and let them fall to the floor with my boxers. I pulled my shirt over my head.

"Please! Please don't," Mackenzie begged.

Before I could take a naked breath, Marcy dropped to her knees and started to suck me off. It felt fine, but not the way I wanted it. None of this was the way I wanted it.

I stared at Mackenzie as I forced my dick deeper into Marcy's mouth. The old me clawed through my chest, trying to burst through. If I let him escape, he would tear mouse to smithereens. He wouldn't fuck her gently like I could. At least, how I imagined I could.

Marcy stood up and went to sit in the rocking chair. The red stain of blood remained from when I'd cut Mackenzie. It glared up at me as Marcy leaned back and put her hand down her pants.

I crawled into bed with Mackenzie. She kicked her legs out at me, but there wasn't enough force behind them anymore. I pinned her thighs down and got between them. Tears streamed down her face, but I kept my gaze on her lips. I had to avoid looking into her eyes. I pulled the fabric down, exposing her breasts. I traced my fingers along her nipples.

Marcy groaned. "None of this foreplay shit. Just fuck her."

I shook my head but obeyed, bunching the gown toward her waist. The heat of what I wanted—what I craved since the moment I saw her—radiated toward me. My cock throbbed at the thought of pushing inside her. I pressed my length against her, leaned over her, and kissed her. She kept her lips pinched together. When I pulled away, balancing on my hands, I made the fatal mistake of looking at her eyes.

Fuck.

Soft. Rounded with sadness. They reached across the open air between us and poured into me. She blinked away the gloss in her eyes as she looked up at me. I couldn't stay hard. She had given up fighting me. Her look softened me in an instant.

Fuck. Fuck!

I kissed her again, spreading her lips with my tongue. I willed myself to get hard again. I *had* to get hard again. I grinded my hips into the warm wetness of her, but I was too limp to enter her.

Marcy made a noise from deep in her throat.

I leaned over Mackenzie. "I'm sorry, mouse," I whispered in her ear before sitting up.

"What the hell is the matter with you?" Marcy screamed as she made her way across the room. She grabbed the pistol off the dresser and aimed it at me. I put my hands up as she came and grabbed my limp cock.

"Guess the sound of the gun cocking isn't enough to stiffen me up this time," I said with a half-smile as she rubbed me.

Marcy took a few steps back. The barrel of the gun stayed level with my chest, shaking as she battled within herself. Her pleasure depended on me fucking someone else. If I couldn't do that, no one was safe.

"Benjamin, what have you done?" Marcy whispered. Her face shifted, going from pissed off house cat to glossy-eyed kitten in the time it took me to draw a breath.

She'd snapped.

"Marcy, think about what you're doing." I was the one pleading now.

"I already did."

She let the barrel drop slightly, and the sound of the gunshot filled the room. I screamed, Mackenzie screamed, and Marcy inhaled sharply. Blood sprayed across the duck pictures, making them look hunted.

I collapsed onto the bed. Crimson liquid flowed over my skin and onto the mattress beneath me. I took shallow breaths. It was all I could manage against the pain. I searched my naked body, desperate to find the source—a bullet hole in my upper arm with frayed skin around its edges.

Marcy walked out of the room and slammed the door. She'd done the damage, but she wasn't woman enough to watch me bleed out.

Fucking coward.

Mackenzie sat up, her free hand over her mouth. Her eyes were wide.

"Oh my god, Benjamin!" she shrieked.

I don't know where it came from inside her. I had nearly raped her. My blood dripped between her legs, covering her in warm crimson.

"You need to sit up," she commanded.

Why does she care if I bleed out on the mattress in front of her? Monsters deserve to get shot.

I sat up, and blood slid down my chest. She looked around the room, searching for something to slow the steady flow. Letting myself go straight to hell where I belonged was a better idea.

"Grab your shirt!" she shouted.

I clutched the skin just beneath my shoulder and the blood spread around my fingers. I couldn't bear to hear her so worked up, so I grabbed my shirt off the floor.

"Now what?" I asked between clenched teeth.

"You have to hold pressure on it. Ball up the shirt and use your other hand to hold it down. Firm pressure."

She sounded like she knew what she was talking about, so I obeyed. I crumpled the shirt between my fingers and shoved it over the wound. I pressed down as hard as I could.

"Jesus!" I groaned, raised my head, and contemplated praying. I was once raised as a Christian, after all. But if there was a god, he wouldn't be coming to my aid.

"Why'd you do that?" she whispered.

"Do what?"

"Not . . . rape me?"

"I just couldn't." I could barely get the words out over the pain.

"Why not?"

She sounded insecure, as if my inability to perform was a reflection of her. Like I wouldn't have fucked her if I met her outside of that house.

I closed my eyes. "You looked at me with that face."

"What face?"

"I don't know. It's this face you make when you're scared. Your eyes get really big, like a whipped puppy, and your lip trembles." I kept my eyes closed, finding comfort behind my eyelids.

"I'm sorry," she whispered.

"Don't be. There's something wrong with me, and I don't know what's going to happen to you because of it. Hell, I don't even know what will happen to me."

I was as much of a captive as she was. My chains were just invisible.

I opened my eyes as Marcy walked into the room. She wouldn't look at me. Mackenzie shied away from her as she unlocked her and ripped her from the bed.

I crawled toward the edge of the mattress. "It's not her fault!"

"Bullshit," Marcy snapped. "She knows what she did. She got in your head. I told you not to let these sluts get into your head. Filthy girls."

I held my breath. mouse did get into my head, but I wanted to let her in. And now we would pay for it.

Chapter Eleven

MACKENZIE

Back in the basement, my head swirled with confusion. I dropped my hands between my legs, thankful I still hadn't lost what he so desperately wanted to take. I ran a hand over the dried blood on the insides of my thighs. His blood. Going into that room, I thought I would be the one left bleeding. I imagined him tearing me to shreds while overcome by his primitive mind. He was the unforgiving predator, and I was his prey. I took a deep breath. For now, I would hold on to the innocence he frothed at the mouth to steal. I just wished I knew *why*.

He didn't seem like the type to get attached. If he thought he had feelings for Marcy, he wouldn't be able to recognize actual feelings if they hit him in the dick.

And what about my own emotions? My mind locked on the memory of straining against the chain as he spread my legs. The thought of his rough touch and primal eyes. Fear coursed through me when he climbed on top of me, but an underlying wave of excitement surged there as well, trying to suck me into the depths. I didn't fear him, though. I feared what would happen next. When his eyes—and cock—softened in front of me, I felt a twinge of something. My body had begun to respond to him, and that was the last thing I ever wanted. That little twinge in my gut was sharp at the end. If I wasn't careful, it would gouge its way through my insides and puncture my soul.

Then Marcy shot him, and I felt the need to help him. But why? A shiver ran through me.

God damn it.

I dropped my forehead against my knees. I still fucking hated him, but wasn't that how Stockholm syndrome began? A confusing attraction to a despicable human?

That place was hell with no answers. No rhyme or reason. It was pointless to try to untangle the mess of their lives. They spoke a foreign language, and I wasn't privy to their dialect. I was in an unfamiliar country. Maybe even another world.

BENJAMIN

I OPENED the door to the basement, balancing a plate in one hand and a glass of water in the other, the liquid sloshing with every step. Her back pressed against the wall. She stared straight ahead. I looked at her, wondering if she was thinking about the bedroom like I was. When she shivered, I knew she was. Bringing food wasn't enough to earn her forgiveness, not that I deserved it.

A dull throb rippled through my shoulder where I'd been shot. Fucking *shot.*

Even though she refused to look at me, I walked over and

squatted down in front of her. I placed the plate and glass on the ground and stood up, wiping the dirt off my hands. Pain throbbed beneath my bandaged arm. I turned to walk away, to go back to the safety of familiarity.

"Benjamin?" she whispered.

I was tempted to respond, but it was safer if I didn't. My feelings were dangerous. I was torn, and I'd never been that way. I'd lost my hold with Marcy. Would she really keep me around any longer? If not, she needed to finish the job the right way.

"I don't understand why you won't talk to me." She looked up at me with wide eyes. She could tell I was shutting her out.

I *had* to. I let myself get weak, and now we both had to pay for my lapse of strength. Her words tugged at my heart. The tone of her voice weaseled into my ears and lodged itself into my temporal lobe—the area of my brain responsible for my feelings of love and fear. I should have put a pillow over her face and fucked her. Got it over with. I was tired of holding her innocence like a glass ball in my hand. If I had just taken her, I wouldn't have been shot. Yeah, she'd have lost some of herself, but at least it would have gotten us off of Marcy's firing line.

I turned away from her, and my expression softened. I had to put up a front around her now, to protect her. Making her hate me was the safest thing for both of us. I could only keep the wolf away by dressing as one myself.

"Eat," I said with forced harshness.

"Yeah," she said. Betrayal was woven within her voice.

Good. That was what she needed to feel. I *did* betray her, as fucked up as that was. I turned around, closed my eyes, and took a deep breath before heading for the stairs.

Damn it.

I spun on my heels and sat down on the ground in front of her, no words daring to leave my lips.

I have no fucking clue why I'm drawn to her. I've never felt anything like this.

I picked up the plate and looked at the chunky, mashed mixture spreading across the surface. I curled my lip at the sight of it. The texture was all wrong. I didn't want to force her to eat it, but she wasn't leaving me with much choice if she refused. I slid it toward her again, hoping it wouldn't come to that.

She dipped her finger into the goop and lifted it, the thin liquid dripping onto the plate. She touched her tongue with her finger and grimaced. She gagged, her throat fighting against her as she shoveled a handful of the meat mixture into her mouth. She swallowed the slop until she reached her limit, and with a quick shake of her head, she put the plate down on the floor.

I was tempted to force her to eat more. She was too thin. My eyes went to the plate, and I curled my lip at what was left of the pink gelatinous pile.

How can I make her eat something I wouldn't?

Aside from the angry gurgling of her stomach, we sat in silence. I checked the time on my watch. It had been almost thirty minutes since she'd eaten. Marcy would get suspicious if I—

She gagged again.

I cocked my head, trying to understand how she was still feeling sick after so much time had passed. *Was the meat rotten?*

She scrambled onto her hands and knees and heaved. She couldn't even reach her bucket before she violently threw up on herself. Red, chunky vomit caked her hair and the front of her gown. She vomited again at the sight of her own puke. I thought her stomach was going to lurch into her throat and out of her mouth from the force. I fought the urge to comfort her. The last thing either of us needed was for Marcy to come down the stairs and see me with my hand patting her back.

She leaned against the wall, turned her head, and vomited again. The stench of the rancid liquid wafted over me. Puke covered her, rolling down her chest and dripping onto her legs.

Thirty minutes? Marcy did something to her food.

She'd done something similar to me once or twice, making me vomit everything, including my childhood memories. There was no release from the pain brought on by ipecac. Just nagging, twisting agony.

She collapsed onto her back with her eyes closed. I didn't leave her side, sitting quietly among the stench with my back against the wall. I sucked air through my mouth, making my breaths heavier than intended.

"Did you know?" she whispered without sitting up.

I lifted an eyebrow. "Did I know what?"

"That she poisoned me?"

"It wasn't poison. It was probably ipecac," I said with a shrug, as if that was any better.

Her head tilted to the side so she could look at me. "Did you know it was in this food?"

"No," I whispered. *I didn't. But I'm not surprised.*

She took a deep breath, inhaling the foul air around her. "She thinks you're attracted to me."

I dropped my gaze, grinding the heel of my shoe into the ground. "Yeah, I know."

"I know? That's all you can say? What does that mean for me?" She raised her voice as she struggled to sit, tempting me to throw a hand across her mouth to shut her up.

"I'm not sure." In the eleven years I'd been in that house, I was never attracted to any of the women. Not the way I was with Mackenzie. I had nothing to compare it to and no way to know how Marcy would deal with it.

"Is she going to kill me?" Her jaw trembled.

I hesitated for too long. Even in the darkness, I could see her muscles tense at my lack of an answer. "I don't know," I said. I looked down at her with pity, as if there was a clock ticking over her head.

Was there?

She threw her hands up. "How do you not know? What's happened before? With others?"

"The same thing that happened to the one beneath the tree," I murmured.

"Which was?"

I wondered if I should tell her the story. Maybe if I did, she'd stay away from me. She'd be scared like she needed to be.

Fuck it.

"I walked down here one day, and she couldn't even lift her head. Her breath was so shallow, I had to watch real closely to even tell she was alive." I grabbed at the toe of my shoe, squeezing it. "She looked at me with this longing, and I knew what it was for. She wanted to die."

Mackenzie swallowed hard. "And?"

"I called to Marcy. She drew her gun, whispered something I couldn't hear, and shot her in the temple. Marcy stood over her until she stopped twitching. Then she told me to clean it up." I dropped my head against the wall. "She took a piece of me with her to the grave."

"How many people are buried out there?"

I rubbed my beard, contemplating if I wanted to tell her the truth, or if she would be more comforted by a lie. "Three." I paused. "And a half."

She drew in a quick breath. "*A half?*"

Her reaction was so strong, I decided she'd be better off

not knowing the full truth. "I'm kidding. There's just three." *Not really much better.*

"You're poorly socialized if you think murder humor is appropriate right now."

I shrugged my shoulders. I *was* poorly socialized.

"What about the others?" she asked.

"I can't talk about that." I lowered my gaze. *I won't talk about that.*

"Why?"

"You and your damn questions." I got to my feet.

"Okay, fine," she whispered, and turned her head away from me.

I sighed, climbed the stairs, and let the door lock behind me. I couldn't bear the smell anymore. I couldn't deal with her questions. Her words forced me into memories I didn't want to remember.

Chapter Twelve

MACKENZIE

I woke to Marcy hovering over me, her inflammatory stare boring into my soul. I jumped, sat up, and scooted against the wall. The noxious smell of urine and mold had somehow faded. Maybe I had become used to it. Marcy leaned down and kept her gaze on me, as if I were an animal on exhibit. I was sick of this life. I was tired, and no amount of sleep would satisfy the exhaustion in my bones.

"I don't like you," Marcy snarled.

"I'm not much of a fan of you either, Marcy."

Her jaw dropped. "This is what I mean. Can't you just be normal?"

I raised my eyebrows and curled my lip at her. "Normal? Nothing and no one in this place is normal! I've given up on trying to be your pet."

"You make waves and cause rifts between Benjamin and me. You're trying to tear us apart!"

"If you want to know why the two of you are coming apart, look in a fucking mirror. You don't need my help.

You're doing a great job of that on your own. Benjamin isn't an equal partner in this, and it's not my fault that he's finally realizing it."

Her eyes widened. "What has he told you?"

"Nothing." I shrugged. "You told me everything I needed to know when you shot him."

Marcy shook her head. "You know what, Mackenzie? I'm going to find out exactly how he feels about you."

She reached for my chain and popped open the lock. Without waiting for me to get to my feet, she started for the stairs. My knees scraped against the concrete. I put my hands on the bottom step, stalling Marcy long enough to get to my feet. She marched us past the bathroom and headed toward the back door. She produced a key from her pocket and unlocked the deadbolt.

Why lock it when I'm secured in the basement?

We stepped into blinding sunlight. I shielded my face as the rays caressed my sickly pale skin. My body jerked forward. Marcy tugged me outdoors like an unwilling dog. Cushiony grass tickled my bare feet. It was a welcome change from the cold, unforgiving concrete. Marcy brought me toward the tree, wrapped the tail of the chain around the trunk, and locked it on itself.

"Benjamin!" Marcy yelled.

"What?" he screamed from inside the house.

Marcy sighed. "Come out here! Now!" She folded her arms across her chest and wiggled her leg.

Benjamin walked into the sunlight. He wiped his hands on a rag and dropped it on the step. He squinted his eyes and looked at us, trying to figure out what fresh hell Marcy had in store. More evidence that he was as much in the loop as I was.

He walked over to Marcy and stood beside her. "What?"

"I just want you to be here for this," Marcy said as she

pulled the revolver out of her waistband. She popped the cylinder out, reached into her pocket, and grabbed six bullets. She took her time loading each one. After closing the cylinder, she spun it around and smiled.

Realization washed over me. With my hands raised toward Marcy, I screamed at her. "Marcy, whoa! No! What are you doing?" I was so sick of begging for things. My virtue. My life. But what choice did I have? I wasn't going to lay down and die. I wasn't the same as the girl beneath my feet.

"You know what I'm doing. You know too much." She pointed the barrel at my head and turned toward Benjamin with a smug grin. "Thanks to him."

"Marcy, we didn't talk about this. You didn't mention killing her," Benjamin said, his hands tucked into his jean pockets. He kept his voice even. If he was concerned, he wasn't showing it.

"I don't need your permission to do anything, Benjamin. There's no point in keeping her any longer." She lowered the pistol to her side. "It's almost as if you're trying to dissuade me."

"I'm not, but maybe we should give it another chance. I wasn't feeling well last time." He shrugged.

"No, I'm not giving her another chance to fuck with us. Look what she's already done." She gestured between us with the barrel of the pistol.

"Help!" I screamed into the rustling trees around us. Birds scattered from the limbs, their wings flapping wildly as they fled. *I wish I had fucking wings.*

"You can scream all you want. There's no one around here for miles on any side." She screamed along with me, mocking my desperation.

It didn't stop me from trying. I gasped, struggling to catch my breath between screams. Marcy raised the gun in the air and pulled the trigger. My mouth slammed shut.

Benjamin stepped in front of Marcy, and she squinted her eyes at him.

What are you doing, Benjamin?

"I don't think we should do this right now." He tried to reason with Marcy, but Marcy wasn't reasonable.

"Get out of the way Benjamin, or the next one will be for you." She pushed past him and set her sights on me again.

BENJAMIN

I COULDN'T PUSH FURTHER. If I did, Marcy would know something was up between us. *Was* there something between us? No. Not anything that went both ways. It was a one-sided infatuation on my part, but that was enough to get the object of my obsession destroyed. If I wanted to save my mouse, I had to keep my distance. I stepped aside and took a couple steps back.

Mackenzie trembled the same way she had in the ice bath. My heart skipped a beat at the sight of her. This was her execution, and it was all my fault. All I had to do was fuck her. I *wanted* to fuck her. Even as I was about to witness her murder, I wanted nothing more than to sink inside her.

God damn it.

"Kneel!" Marcy commanded.

Mackenzie hesitated. Her eyes shifted to me, pleading for help. If I felt anything for her, now was the time to show it. I could overpower Marcy, take the gun, and let her go. I wouldn't let myself leave alive, but I could free her. I willed myself to act, but my feet were rooted to the earth.

I couldn't save her.

She closed her eyes and dropped to her knees. Marcy

raised the gun and aimed at her head. Mackenzie sobbed, every tear bringing her closer to the realization that this was the only escape she would have. And maybe it was. When she quieted and a smile crept across her face, I knew she was smiling at the thought of being free.

I'd been there more times than I cared to admit.

I screamed inside. I wanted to dive in front of Mackenzie and shield her, but if I jumped in front of that bullet, I would be free, not her. My little mouse. Could I even call her that anymore? There was nothing meek about her.

The need to preserve my own life kept me still as stone. My stomach tightened at the click of the gun as Marcy prepared to fire it. I stared at her finger, still in a neutral position and not yet on the trigger. Clammy sweat slicked my palms. I wanted to yell and reason with Marcy, but I couldn't. Not without confirming my attraction to Mackenzie. She was doomed either way.

Marcy turned to look at me. She read my body language, seeking the answers to her questions. I kept my face blank. Finding what she needed, she turned back to Mackenzie and curled her finger around the trigger. I crammed my fingers into my ears, trying to drown out Mackenzie's screams. They pierced through my chest and stirred something foreign inside me. It should have been me on the receiving end of a bullet to the head. I didn't deserve to live. I didn't deserve to keep going. Mackenzie did.

I closed my eyes. When the echo of the gunshot quieted, Mackenzie continued to scream. I searched her body with my eyes, looking for the gush of blood or the fatal hole. I turned to Marcy and dropped my hands from my ears. She grinned from ear to ear.

"Blanks!" she squealed.

Are you fucking kidding me?

My jaw dropped. She managed to surpass a whole new

level of low. Even for us. She walked over, placed the gun back in her waistband, and wrapped her arms around me. I couldn't return the affection. I was in too much shock.

"Marcy, what were you thinking?" I whispered.

"I needed to see if you had feelings for her. And I need her to respect me. You should have heard the things she said to me."

Mackenzie fell backwards with her arm stuck straight up because of the taut chain. She sobbed hysterically. Was it because her life had been spared? Or because her freedom had been denied? Were they tears of joy or tears of sorrow?

"What the fucking fuck!" she yelled between sobs. Her tears washed away some of the grime on her face. Pee dribbled down her thighs, the gown offering no coverage.

I put my arms around Marcy and looked past her. I needed to play her game. I glanced at Mackenzie. She needed to play too.

When Marcy pulled that trigger and shot me, I wanted to grovel at her feet for her forgiveness. When the gun went off this time, she pulled the trigger on my feelings for her. She wasn't the person I once knew. She had changed.

Or had I?

Chapter Thirteen

MACKENZIE

The unwelcome sound of Benjamin's steps drew closer as he came down the stairs, a Styrofoam plate gripped between his fingers.

What's the point of eating? My stomach growled.

"Are we going to talk about what happened yesterday?" I whispered as I took the plate from his hands.

He shook his head and sat down in front of me. I crossed my legs to be modest, the gown riding up and leaving me exposed. I set the plate down on the ground and looked at the wall.

What's the point of food if it only keeps you alive like this? "Has she done this before?" I asked.

Benjamin's gaze poured into mine. "No. Well, yes, but never with blanks," he said. "She used the real thing." Despite the darkness in his eyes and the intensity of his stare, he took his shirt off and gestured at my lap. Something told me he wasn't offering modesty for my benefit alone.

I reached for it, but hesitated. "Are you sure you want to do that? I'm so gross."

"Yeah, you are." He kept the shirt extended toward me.

I took it and draped it over my lap, giving myself the coverage I craved. The scars on his body snagged my eyes and held them in place. They covered his skin like contour lines on a map. His chest was under muscled, but his arms were still strong. His ribs protruded slightly and stretched his skin. He wasn't a picture of health, as if Marcy was in control of his meals as well. Maybe she kept him weak intentionally. Allowed to thrive, Benjamin would have been a force to be reckoned with. He was—as much as I hated to admit it—handsome. In a rugged kind of way.

"Why would she do a mock execution? It doesn't make sense," I said, dropping my gaze. I played with the soft fabric of his shirt.

Benjamin shrugged, letting his shoulder drop. "I don't know. She isn't acting normal."

"Normal? Like that could ever describe the woman holding me captive."

"There's a certain level of crazy that is normal for her, yes." He almost let a smirk cross his face.

I stared at him blankly.

He reached out and grabbed my scarred hands. "Like this." He touched the scars before letting go of my fingers. "This was her normal crazy line." He held one hand out in front of him with his palm facing the floor. "And this is where she is right now." He raised his second hand well above the other.

I smiled at his animated hand gestures—my first genuine smile since the nightmare began. I looked at the scars winding up my wrists, and the corners of my mouth drifted downward. Benjamin's arms held me as the water scalded my already burned flesh. Benjamin held the knife that created the marks on my thighs. My body tensed.

"Your smart mouth got you those," he said flatly.

The sudden curveball in his tone made me sit up taller. My mouth dropped open. "Excuse me? My what?" I pushed a thick clump of hair behind my ear. The vomit had dried and hardened, giving my locks a crunchy texture.

Benjamin played with his fingers. "Your mouth. You called her a cunt." His tone was matter of fact, as if I'd had it coming to me.

"Are you victim blaming right now?" I snapped. *Fuck you.*

Benjamin shook his head and met my eyes. "No, but I need you to keep your mouth shut."

I tightened my lips at his words. Silence fell on us, thick and heavy.

"You can still talk to me. You just can't keep fighting Marcy," he said. He brushed his hand through his hair.

"And why should I stop fighting? Isn't that what you're supposed to do in these circumstances? Fight?"

"I can't protect you anymore, mouse. I have nothing to bargain with at this point. I can hardly get it up anymore." He put his face in his hands. "If I can't please her, I'll end up under that tree too. Once she kills me, who do you think is next? Don't be stupid."

"You think it's better to just give in and let her own us?" I rose to my knees, the concrete rubbing my bare skin. The chain rattled as I leaned toward him.

Benjamin leaned away from me. "Yes, because I loved her."

"You loved her. Past tense."

"No." He hesitated. "I do love her. She's all I've ever known. She's like a mother to me."

"Well, that's gross."

"You wouldn't understand," he whispered.

"Try me." I sat back on my heels with a deflated breath.

Our heads snapped toward the door at the click of disengaging locks. Benjamin stood up. His eyes darted from me to the stairs as he grabbed his shirt and slipped it back on. Marcy's heavy, uneven footsteps echoed on the floor above.

"Benjamin?" she yelled.

He picked up the plate, dumped some of the food into my bucket, and headed toward the stairs. "Coming! Just fed her." He turned to look at me again before taking the steps two at a time.

I took a deep breath. There was something mildly enchanting about him, but I couldn't tell if it was because he was the last man alive in my new little world or if it was something more. He had every opportunity and encouragement to take me in that bedroom, yet his mind and body denied the act. An ultimate betrayal that sank deeper than the mind. That said something.

I looked down at my vomit-encrusted gown and groaned. The scent of bile and urine wafted throughout the basement. *No wonder he couldn't get hard for me.* I pushed my thoughts of self-pity away, unwilling to rate my attractiveness based on my rapeability.

I lay back on the cold concrete and turned my head to the right. An off-color stain on the floor looked back at me, and I wondered if someone else took their last breath in the exact spot where I lay. *I'm almost positive they have. This chain is only so long.* I tried to tug the skimpy gown over my thighs, but it only reached the edges of my ass cheeks.

There was a loud crashing sound on the floor above me. A heavy thud. As I looked up at the beams crossing along the ceiling, my thoughts wandered to Benjamin. Had he stood up for himself? Did one of them hit the ground? I held my breath and listened. For a while, it was quiet. Then footsteps clobbered the floor again, and an upstairs door slammed. A few minutes passed before more footsteps shook the rafters above my head. Benjamin appeared in the doorway and came toward me.

"So, there's a situation." He let out a sigh.

I raised my brow. "Like?"

"Marcy went to the hospital."

My eyes widened. Hope warmed my gut. If she was gone, maybe I could convince Benjamin to let me go. "The hospital? Why? How?"

"She has diabetes. She goes into ketoacidosis every so often. Starts vomiting everywhere. She ends up in the hospital for days, sometimes even a week." His lips played at the edges of a smile.

"If this has happened before, why are you still here? Let's get the hell out of here." The thought of freedom allowed me enough energy to stand on tired legs.

"I can't." Benjamin kicked at the ground beneath his feet. "She drives herself to the hospital, and she always locks the door from the outside on her way out. I've been waiting for a long time for something to go different, but it never does."

My jaw relaxed. Hope waned, freezing my insides. "The windows?"

"Metal bars. Benjamin did a great job of making this place inescapable," he said, slipping a trembling hand through his dark hair.

"I thought you were Benjamin?"

"I am." He shook his head.

"Explain."

He took a deep breath, and his eyes locked on mine. "Benjamin was Marcy's husband."

"Was?"

"Yeah, he drank himself to death in the living room about ten years ago," Benjamin said as he traced the scars on his wrist.

"Wait, so who are you?"

He hesitated, as if unable to separate the two identities he held. "I'm Dylan."

"Dylan?" My mind raced. "How the fuck did you become Benjamin?"

"When her husband died, she needed . . . well, a new one," he said.

"So, she abducted you?"

His eyes dropped. "No, I was already here. My sister and I walked into this house eleven years ago and never left."

All the nightmares had been built from lies.

BENJAMIN

"WHAT HAPPENED?" she asked.

I wished she hadn't, because I didn't want to remember. I tried to let go of the memories of my sister. The rape, abuse, and death of Della. Benjamin had been something conjured up from horror stories. Della and I faced such unspeakable torture at the hands of that drunk piece of shit.

"That's a story best left untold," I mumbled.

Mackenzie stared at me, set on having answers whether I wanted to supply them or not. She'd pester me every time I came to the basement, just as she had with my name. Maybe a part of me wanted to tell it.

I cleared my throat. "We were selling stupid raffle tickets. Going door to door. Marcy spotted us walking and said she'd buy the rest of the tickets, but we had to ride with her to get the money from her house. I trusted my sister when she got in the damn car. I would have followed her anywhere, even into the jaws of this beast. When we got here, Marcy locked the door, and Benjamin took us into the basement and locked us up."

"Was Marcy like this back then?" she asked.

I pulled a cigarette from my pocket and lit it, needing to keep my hands busy. The cigarette sizzled as I inhaled. Memories swirled around me, sucking me into darkness. "No, never. Benjamin was violent enough for the both of them. He would beat on us, hang us from the rafters, rape . . ." I shook my head. "He raped Della and made me watch. All the damn time. He almost made me do it too, but Marcy stopped it."

Her spirit haunted me. Sometimes I could still feel her arms around my torso, embracing me. I also felt her icy whispers in my ear as I inflicted the same pain she endured onto others.

"Did they . . ."

"No, they never did that to me. I wasn't their thing. Marcy got off on Benjamin with the girls." I swallowed hard, tasting the smoke at the back of my throat.

Watching was a guilty pleasure which worsened over time for Marcy, as if the more it happened, the more she needed to see to feel the same high.

"How long was she alive?" she asked, leaning closer to me.

"Three years, maybe."

"And they abused her the whole time?"

"She was a goddamn living punching bag. When she wasn't being fucked, she was getting beat. Benjamin loved to hate her. She tended to make great escapes, like the one you tried. She had a smart mouth too." A tight smirk pulled at my lips. "Benjamin was so cruel, I wasn't sure he was human until he died. Aside from a brief seven-month break, he abused her every day."

Mackenzie put a hand over her mouth. "She wasn't . . ."

"Yep. Pregnant. She went into labor, screaming and sweating for days, but the baby didn't come. Broken pelvis that healed wonky is my guess. They'd broken every bone in her body within those three years. Her last words to me were an apology for making me get in the car. What a stupid thing to apologize for." I scoffed. "I still don't know exactly how she died. Marcy took me upstairs and locked me in her room. When I came back down, Della was gone."

"Three and a half bodies. That's the half?" Mackenzie sighed and drew her knees toward her chest. I tried to keep from staring at the shadow between her legs.

Not the time.

I shrugged.

"Why did they keep you?"

I lit another cigarette as soon as I smothered the first. "That was when the fun really began. I was a threat to Benjamin before I even had hair on my chin. He brutalized me." I lifted my shirt to show the deep scars on my back. "He would burn me, whip me, break my fingers. He hung me from the rafters for days, my feet hardly able to touch the floor. He probably would have killed me if it wasn't for Marcy. She got really attached to me." I took a deep breath. "She loved me."

"None of this is love, you know. You have to know that." She reached out to me and touched my shoulder. "You could take her out. Help us escape."

I shook my head before she even finished her sentence. "I can't hurt Marcy. She's the only one who's ever taken care of me. She's all I have."

"That's insane. Do you hear yourself? How can you be attached to the woman who held you captive?" She flailed her arms toward the door.

I sat on my knees and fisted her hair, tugging her up. Her breath halted as I pulled her body into me, and she looked up with more curiosity than fear. I was so fucking frustrated. The tornado of emotions she stirred up coupled with the lack of sex . . . I was starving for her. I could lay her down, spread her thighs, and take what I needed. But the way she looked up at me—like I was something more than I was yesterday—made me drop my hand from her hair. She couldn't wrap her mind around it, but when I was so badly beaten I thought I was going to die, Marcy was the one who took care of me. I didn't expect her to understand our relationship. I hardly understood it myself.

"It's not so insane to find comfort in your captor," I said.

"I most definitely haven't." She shook her head. "I don't hate you, but what I feel is still very far from being attached." She scoffed and sat back on her heels.

Instead of taking what I wanted, I showed restraint once again. I left the basement. She could keep her innocence for the time being, but not forever.

Chapter Fourteen

MACKENZIE

Benjamin walked into the basement, no locks rattling on the door this time. The silence was eerie and almost uncomfortable. He came over and squatted beside me, breathing through his mouth as he looked at me.

"Morning," he said.

"What?" I groaned and sat up.

"I found the key to your lock," he said with a tight-lipped smile.

I climbed to my knees, flashing my eyes up at him.

"Before you get all excited, I don't have the door keys." He reached down, took my arm, and helped me to my feet. His full lips crept into a sly smile. "What would you trade for some freedom?"

My heart sank. "Really?" I folded my arms across my chest and looked away from him.

"Yeah. If Marcy comes back before I can get you back down here, we're both inexcusably fucked. I want something that would make it all worth it." The gravelly tone of his voice brought a small twinge of excitement into my stomach, knotting it in a way I couldn't understand.

"God forbid you be nice for nothing in return." I pushed down the excited feeling, tucking it away where it belonged. Somewhere that would never see the light of day.

"Nothing in this life is free, mouse. Especially *this* life."

My cheeks flamed red, spreading down my chest and settling inside my angry heart. The hateful words I wanted to say became lodged in my throat. I refused to meet his eyes, choosing instead to stare at the dark stain on the concrete. I considered dropping to my knees for some freedom, which was the sad part. What was the point of maintaining my virtue when every day was potentially my last?

"Fine." He reached out and brushed hair away from my cheek. "Don't get all worked up."

I jerked away from his touch.

He unlocked the manacle from my wrist. It separated with a scrape of aged metal, the sound both haunting and reassuring. I rubbed at my sore wrist. The constant contact of the steel against sweat had worn down my skin.

"Are we going to stay in the basement and enjoy the beautiful landscape, or are we going upstairs?" he asked. His sarcasm rivaled mine.

I was a feral animal released from a cage, too shell-shocked to make my own decisions. I nodded and fumbled forward on unsteady legs. Without the heavy weight of the chain on my right arm, I felt unbalanced.

"I have so many questions," I said as we reached the top of the stairs.

"I can't guarantee I'll answer them," he said.

"What do I call you? Benjamin or Dylan?"

He turned toward me, his lips in a tight line. "Benjamin. If you slip up, one or both of us are as good as dead."

I nodded.

I stood in the hallway, my eyes roving over everything. I wiggled my toes on the hardwood floors, cold to the touch. The pale-yellow bedroom stood on my right, and seeing the bloodstained duck sent a shiver coursing through me. I turned to the left. I couldn't look through that open door for another second.

Two plates sat on the table in the small kitchen. Benjamin pulled out a chair and sat down. He gestured toward the second chair. "I made breakfast, but it's probably not great."

I walked over and took a seat. The pancakes were overdone, the edges nearly black, but I didn't care. It was food, and better yet, it was my choice to eat.

"It was all we had left until Marcy can go shopping again." He picked up his fork and looked down.

Excited to hold a utensil in my hand, I shoveled the pancakes into my mouth. Sweet and sticky syrup dripped down my chin.

Benjamin stared at me.

"What? I haven't eaten any real food since Marcy kidnapped me, or have you forgotten?" I pointed to my stained gown. "So you're going to have to excuse my shitty table manners."

"Yeah," he whispered, bringing food to his mouth.

I took another massive bite and looked around the room. A deadbolt lock stared back at me from the front door. It had been installed in reverse, with the keyhole on the interior and the hand turn on the outside. Thick black metal barred the windows. He hadn't lied. There was no way out of there.

"Do you know where Marcy keeps the keys?" I asked.

"For the exterior doors?"

I nodded.

"I don't know where she hides them when she's here, but when she's gone, she keeps them with her. Don't even think about searching for them. I've tried it before. She'll notice if the smallest thing is out of place when she gets back, and then we're fucked."

I eyed the black bars on the windows. "What about those?"

A sly smile pulled his lips up at the corners of his mouth. "Go ahead and give it a try."

I pushed back from the table and went to the window. Placing both hands around a single bar, I threw back my weight. It didn't give. Not even a little. A laugh escaped Benjamin, and I whirled to face him.

"What's so fucking funny?" I snapped.

"If I can't move those things, what makes you think you can? You probably weigh less than one hundred pounds soaking wet. Come finish your food."

He wasn't wrong. I was skin and bones, with no muscle to move much more than a textbook, let alone iron bars. With a frustrated groan, I returned to the table and took my seat in front of the plate of cold eggs.

"How long have I been here?" I asked.

"Almost two months. Give or take." Benjamin shrugged.

I had to mourn my life before I was dead, but he treated it like talking about the weather.

"Two months?" I looked down at my ribs. They protruded through the gown's thin fabric. Two months seemed accurate.

"I want to let you shower," he said with a side glance, "but it's a risk you need to decide you want to take. It could end up being a death sentence for you."

"It doesn't matter. You already said if you can't get hard and use me, I'm good as dead. I would rather die clean than covered in old vomit and piss."

He hesitated and let out a sigh. "Come on. There's no way I'm going to avoid punishment for this, you know."

He brushed a frustrated hand through his hair and led me

toward the bathroom. I stripped off the gown before I even crossed the threshold. Benjamin cocked his head, taking in my naked form. He wasn't very gentlemanly. With a flurry of hands, I pushed him into the hall and shut the door behind him.

The rusted handles squeaked when I turned on the water. I climbed into the old yellow tub, sat down, and let the chilly stream pour down my body. Goosebumps raced across my bare skin. As the water crawled toward warmth, I let out a contented sigh. The grime slid away.

In the light of the bathroom, I looked at my hands—a reminder of my abuse. Burned. Beaten. Scalded. Sexually assaulted. A single tear fell and mixed with the water streaming down my face. I turned up the hot water and let the heat attack and redden my skin.

The cracked bar of soap and the small bottle of shampoo taunted me. Benjamin hadn't said I couldn't use them, but the scent would betray our secret. He'd done me a favor by allowing me to rinse away the dirt and vomit. I would return the favor by doing what I could to cover our tracks. No soap. No shampoo.

I turned off the water, stood, and stepped over the side of the tub. A large nightgown sat on the sink. I never even heard him come in. The gown reminded me of the yellow bedroom, and my stomach clenched.

I used my hand to wipe the cloudy mist away from the mirror, exposing my distorted reflection. Sunken and haunted blue eyes stared back at me. I looked down at my chest—the only part of me still left with any amount of fat. I reached for the gown and put it over my head. The fabric fell toward my knees. I lifted my arms out to the sides to accentuate just how big it was on me.

This feels safe.

I opened the door and walked toward the living room,

leaving cautious wet footprints behind me. Benjamin sat on the couch. The only seat in the room was on the same couch as him. Near him. I felt like a lamb walking into the cage of a lion. When he didn't acknowledge me, I sat down and tried to forget about the predator's teeth beside me. There was an open cushion between us, but it wasn't enough distance. If he wanted to devour me, there'd be nothing I could do to keep myself from ending up inside him. Or him inside me.

He watched the TV, the screen's light reflecting in his dark eyes. I looked down at the stained hardwood floor where Marcy poured the water on my hands. Memories flooded me. Benjamin had held me down. His strong arms could have made me feel safe. Instead, they facilitated pain. I looked at him and tried to untangle the man from the monster.

"We're going to get fucking murdered for this, mouse," he said.

"Then we better make the best of it while we can," I said with a strained smile.

"Yeah, I guess so." He shook his head, struggling with regret over allowing me to have some freedom. Tension spilled into his legs, and they jiggled up and down as he continued watching the television.

I stared at him, taking in his features. He sat silently, chuckling at times over the video clips in the show. His deep brown eyes squinted slightly each time he smiled. His teeth were nice, despite his circumstances. His rolled-up sleeve exposed the old scars covering his arms. Even with everything I knew about him, he was so . . . human . . . ish.

I pulled my legs onto the couch and lay down. It wasn't comfortable, but it felt heavenly compared to the concrete floor. My gown fell past my knees. Benjamin looked at me with a side glance every so often.

"How will you know when Marcy is coming home?" I asked, toying with my gown.

"I won't know until she's unlocking that door. If we're lucky, I'll hear the car in the driveway first."

"Doesn't give us much time, huh?"

"Not at all," he said with a shake of his head.

He looked at me as if he expected me to ask to go back to the basement, but I didn't. I relaxed into the stiff, dingy fabric of the couch and put my arm above my head, embracing the lack of chain.

"Ok, I have to ask." I sat up, scooting back toward the arm of the couch.

"What?" he asked with a small smirk.

"How did she force you to rape women?"

Benjamin's smirk turned into a frown as his gaze met mine. He lifted the sleeve of his shirt and exposed the scarred wound on his shoulder. "With this promise," he said. "I often wondered if it was just an empty threat. If she would actually shoot me if I told her no. Clearly, she would have." He rubbed the skin of his arm. "She'll kill me the next time I refuse anything. This was a warning."

"If she loved you, she wouldn't hurt you," I whispered.

"That's not true." He drew a long breath. "I hurt you. Sometimes we have no choice but to hurt people."

"There's always a choice."

"Is there?" He rubbed his shoulder and looked away from me.

I tried to process his words. Did I find them offensive or flattering? On one hand, he seemed to care about me. On the other, it didn't matter if he did. Neither of our feelings mattered.

"How can you get off during that? Even though you didn't want to do it?" I asked with genuine curiosity. I couldn't wrap my mind around taking someone against their will. To steal the innermost part of them and rip their identity away with every thrust.

His lips moved while he tried to figure out how to say what he wanted in a way that didn't make him sound terrible, but there wasn't one. There was nothing he could say that would make me feel better about his past.

"Once the act was in motion, it still felt good." He shrugged.

"That's awful," I whispered, horrified at the idea of finding enjoyment in something you didn't want to do in the first place. *If he didn't want to do it.*

"I know it is. I became Benjamin in those moments. Like he'd taken control of me. I ended up getting off on the begging and fear." He furrowed his brows. "But I know it's not me. I know I would never take a woman against her will had I not wound up here."

I scoffed. "How do you know?"

He gestured toward me. "I had your half-naked body in front of and against me," he said with a sultry tone. "Your begging words in my ears. God. I wanted you so bad I could taste you. Taste what you were made of. What was inside you. I wanted all of you, every inch of you. But I didn't want it like that." He looked me in the eyes, boring into my soul. "That's how I know. If I was like Benjamin, it would have played out like every other time there's been a woman beneath me. I'd have fucked you till I broke you."

Seduction dripped from his full lips. Such ravenous syllables. I shifted my weight onto my other hip, disgusted by the odd tingle between my legs. I didn't want him to break me, but some hidden part of me wanted to know what it felt like to be taken by him. To allow him to take me.

For a moment, the living room blurred into a forest in the middle of the woods. I had the freedom to run—to take off and leave him to chase me—but my feet were planted, curiosity rooting me to the earth. I had so much more I wanted to know. About him. About this. All of it.

"What did Marcy get out of it?" I asked.

"She would get herself off while watching me." He swallowed hard. "But before I finished, she'd stop me and suck me. She loved the taste of me after I fucked someone else. She would finish me off by getting on top of me and using me."

"That's fucked. What a nice treat for you after all the raping," I said.

"I'm still a man, mouse. What do you want me to do?" He shrugged. He fucking *shrugged!*

Men don't do this. Not like this.

The ache between my legs dulled. *What the hell is wrong with me? He's despicable. He's a rapist!* My cheeks flushed red, and I turned away from him.

"A blowjob is better than a bullet. If I have to fuck to stay alive, that's not the worst trade off," he stated, as if reading my thoughts.

"Except you couldn't fuck, and now she's punishing *me* for it," I snapped.

"Are you honestly mad that I didn't rape you?" Benjamin cocked an eyebrow. His seductive smile caught me off guard.

I couldn't answer. Internally, I was gridlocked and confused. It wasn't that I wanted to be raped, but his inability to do so made me feel three parts relieved and one part undesirable. I didn't want him to rape me, but some sick piece of myself wanted him to *want* me.

He stood up, leaned over me, and grabbed my arms, pinning them above my head. His face was so close to mine, our lips were nearly touching. His warm breath rolled over me, and I felt a twitch of nervous excitement.

"I could change that, mouse," he growled—a gravelly noise from deep within his chest. "I could fuck you right now. Show you just how much I want to tear into you. To break you. To feel your heartbeat through your pussy."

I tensed up. The squint in his eyes made him look so hungry. He was starving. "Benjamin," I whispered. My lips were tight and unwelcoming.

"I'm just kidding. Relax." He smirked and climbed off me.

"What's wrong with you?"

Was he trying to flirt with me?

I racked my brain. Flirting using threats of force wasn't socially acceptable. Being trapped in that house for a decade had left him with zero social skills. Watching him try to flirt —if that's what it was—was like watching the goddamn grim reaper trip and land on his own scythe on his way to collect a soul. Uncomfortable as fuck. I was embarrassed *for* him.

I sat up and scooted my back against the arm of the couch. "Would you do it if it meant she would keep you alive?"

Benjamin sat silent for a few moments. I almost thought he wouldn't answer, but his words finally broke the silence. "I'd like to say no."

"But you can't say no?"

"I don't know what's going to happen. I've never seen her act the way she does with you, so I have no idea how she'll react when she gets back. Would I fuck you if it meant I'd live another day? Possibly. I want to say no, but I don't know that I can. The only thing I know is that things are going to get really bad soon. For both of us. If there's a gun to my head, I hope you know that anything I do to you is not by choice."

I sucked in my cheeks and shook my head, averting my gaze again. "Wow. Okay. Here I am, thinking I could trust you."

He kneeled on the floor next to the couch, grabbed my arm, and pulled me toward him. "Don't trust me. Don't *ever* trust me. It's better if you don't, because I don't trust myself.

I can't think straight around you. You fuck me up." He groaned.

I exhaled and shook my arm out of his grasp. His words made me twitch again. The desire on his tongue called to me, and I hated him for that.

I looked up at him. I *was* a mouse, stumbling into the veiled coil of a snake's body. Would he strike? What a stupid way to tempt the beast.

Chapter Fifteen

MACKENZIE

Without thinking, I bit into my lower lip. He watched me with a frustrated inhale. The heat of tension radiated between us. He fisted my hair, drawing me into him with a rough and sure grasp. His breath rolled over my lips. I looked up at him, and a low growl came from his throat.

"Fuck," he said as he released my hair. "I want to kiss you, but it's a bad idea."

My cheeks flushed with heat at his words. There was a throb between my legs, followed by a pang of guilt. *Don't even think about it.*

Too late. I thought about it.

"I want you to kiss me." The words came out before I could stop them.

Benjamin leaned over me, pressing me against the couch. "You better be sure that's what you want, mouse, because I'm not going to be able to stop once I have my mouth on you."

I bit my lip again. *If I give myself willingly, he can't take it from me. All that he held over me would be gone.*

His lips grabbed mine in a hungry embrace, fiery and unexpected. His hand crawled up my thigh, wasting no time. I took a deep breath and grabbed his wrist. I needed to halt what I set in motion. He was on a crash course, and I was laying across the damn road.

My fingers raced along his arms and grazed scars that looked like scratch marks permanently etched into his flesh. Fingernails could have made those marks . . .

I pulled away from him. "Are these from the women?"

"Yes," he said, and pressed his lips to my neck.

Oh god.

I grabbed his wrist more firmly, straining against his strength. "Stop, Benjamin." I tried to push him away, but he laced a rough hand through my hair. "Stop!" I yelled.

He sat up. "What did I say to you? I don't want to stop. I told you not to start something you couldn't finish."

I sat up and scooted away from him. I couldn't imagine the amount of pain and fear he inflicted on someone to cause them to dig so permanently into his skin. Five reasons why I should *not* sleep with him.

"We should stop," he said as he scooted back to his side of the couch. His eyes flickered with anger. He didn't seem mad at *me,* but he was upset. His cheeks pulsed as his jaw clenched. "You know, Marcy always told me I'm too ugly and scarred up to be with anyone but her. Guess she was right."

I shook my head. "That's not true," I whispered.

Benjamin wasn't ugly. He was rugged and feral. He was scarred. But so was I.

"You can't stomach me because you can see what I've done." He lifted his arms, exposing the tough pink tissue. "These scars brand me as a monster, so you were right about that. There's no place for me besides this house with her."

I looked down and played with the skirt of the gown. "I don't think you're a monster. I wouldn't have let you kiss me if I still thought that." I meant it. He was misguided as fuck, but he wasn't the monster I once thought he was.

"You'd let me take your precious pussy? After everything you've seen and everything I've done to you?" He climbed over me. "Do you know what a bad idea that is? Besides getting in our car, it'd be the stupidest thing you've ever done." His breath rolled over mine. "Do you know how much I could hurt you? I could rip you to shreds and still get off as I wore your blood." His hand touched my cheek—a soft caress against his brewing frustration.

He didn't mean those words. He wanted me to stay away from him and not allow him inside me. Allow. If he didn't scare me off with his words, he'd end up hurting me. Maybe he was more worried that if he slept with me, he *wouldn't* hurt me. That would change everything. I wanted to know what waited inside of him as much as he wanted to know what my insides felt like.

I looked up, refusing to shrink away from him. His words were fire, but instead of hurting me, they warmed me. I lifted my mouth to his and kissed him. He snaked his hand around the back of my neck and pulled me into him. His hand reached down and found the notch of my hip bone, squeezing. His touch sent a shock wave through my body—a unique feeling of fear and excitement that drew me to him. I was the opposite pole of his magnet—a pull that neither of us could fight against.

"If you want me to make love to you, mouse, I can't," he whispered against my mouth. His words were woven with lust and untamed frustration.

"Just follow my pace," I whispered.

"I can't. I want to devour you. I need to fuck you." His

voice was sultry but intimidating, warning me that he held back with every breath he took.

"You will. You just have to wait." I covered his hands with mine, burying them further into my bones.

He growled. "I can't wait a second longer to learn what you feel like. If it's anything like I imagined"—he rubbed a hand down my side and gripped my ass—"you're done for. I'll ravage your body until you don't recognize yourself."

His pushy hands raced along my skin. His eyes grew dark and began to twist into the eerily familiar form I'd seen before. They belonged to another man entirely.

I grabbed his hands and steadied them. "Look at me," I said, mustering the strength to talk him down. "You will not fuck me like you fucked any of them."

His gaze met mine, and he gave me a half-nod, as if he were unsure. Being with a woman who desired him was unnatural for him. He took a deep breath, loosening his grip on my ass as he leaned down to kiss me again. His beard rubbed the soft skin of my chin. He pulled away and stood up. He rushed to unbutton his jeans, letting them fall to the floor with his boxers as he stepped out of them. When he tried to climb back between my legs, I stopped him.

"Shirt too," I said as I tugged at the fabric.

"You don't need to see my chest to fuck me," he snarled.

"Just do it. I'm not hiding my scars, am I?" I lifted my hands toward him.

He groaned but stood back up. He lifted his shirt over his head, exposing the mosaic of scars on his chest, stomach, and arms.

"You're staring," he said.

"Yes, but not why you think."

It was inhuman how much abuse his body had handled, but I was in awe of his masculinity, not his scars. When I touched my healed wounds, it brought me back to that moment, feeling the pain as if it were happening again. I couldn't imagine the agony he felt if he was anything like me —always reliving my most painful moments.

He sat down on the couch, his eyes roving over me. "Now you."

I nodded and stood up, grabbing the bottom of my gown as I rose. I lifted the fabric past my hips and over the taut flesh of my waist. I lifted until I exposed my breasts. With a final yank, I pulled it over my head and dropped it to the ground beside me. Had we been in another situation, it would have been sexy.

Unable to look away, he stared at me. The haunting, familiar look returned to his dark eyes. The hunger. I tensed as he growled and pulled me onto his lap. He was hard beneath me, my skin against his. His nails raked my sides, and his cock twitched.

"Benjamin!"

I tried to push his hands away. He wasn't himself when he got to that point. He knew it, and I knew it. The blood rushed to his cock, leaving nothing for his mind.

"I told you this was a bad idea." His dark irises absorbed every inch of my body. "Just seeing you like this. Naked and willing. It's making me desperate. I'd do anything to feel how much of me you could take. Would I make my little mouse cry or come?"

I'd never had anyone want me so viscerally that their body trembled. The trembling wasn't from fear; it was something deep and dark. It was an animalistic desire from living in a world where you took what you wanted.

He laid me down on my back and pinned me beneath him. He throbbed against my thigh and growled against my neck before kissing me. With a careless motion, he grabbed his cock in his hand and threatened to take me. It felt too familiar.

Panic rose into my chest, cutting off my breath. "Benjamin!" I cursed myself for pleading with him, knowing it just made him harder and hungrier. "You need to slow down."

He dropped his head into the crook of my neck and exhaled. He released his grip on himself and sat down with a heavy breath.

"Fuck! We can't do this. I'm going to hurt you!" He punched the couch cushion, and the metallic thud of old coils answered his frustration.

"No, you aren't. Look at me. I'm not scared of you."

His gaze snapped to mine. "You should be. All I've ever done is hurt women like you! I'm what horror movies are made of. I'm the thing under the bed."

I reached out my hand. "Hey, you said I'm different, right?" I scooted toward him, grabbing one of his hands and placing it between my legs. "Touch me. If you feel like you're getting stuck in this mindset you're used to, do something different."

He took a deep breath and began exploring the soft, warm flesh between my thighs. He leaned over me as his fingers found my wetness, a slick and confused reaction to his words. He pushed his fingers inside me. A low groan slipped past his lips as he placed them against mine. I moaned against his mouth. He took my hand and put it on the warm skin of his cock. He throbbed the moment I wrapped my hand around him, like he'd been dreaming of my touch. He withdrew his fingers and brought them up to me. He pushed them into my mouth, pulling at my lower lip as I took them out.

"How do you expect me to control myself when you do shit like that?" He growled.

I smiled and climbed onto his lap. Heat radiated from his cock. My hips moved without any prompting, grinding along the length of him. He twitched as I curled my hips upward, grazing the tip of his cock before rocking back. I reached down and guided him inside me. He filled me completely.

My hips fought against the immovable pressure of his grasp. I wanted to ride him, but he just wanted to be buried inside me.

"Just let me fuck you. You'll have your chance. I promise," I whispered.

I lifted my body until my chest grazed his mouth, and I lowered my hips again. My moans disappeared into his thick hair. I wrapped my arms around his neck and grinded my hips forward and backward, rubbing myself on his pelvis. His hands squeezed my hips again, desire exploding from his fingertips.

My hips rocked, and he bucked his to meet mine. Moans rolled over my tongue and past my loose lips. He grabbed a fistful of my hair, craning my neck and devouring the skin of my throat. His body trembled, ready to detonate. A ticking bomb. I kept his thighs pinned under me, trying to turn back the clock and remain in the moment. Pleasure radiated through my body, and the source was a smoldering fire between my legs.

For the first time since I climbed into a car on a rainy night, I was in control.

I drew a deep breath. "I'm going to come, Benjamin," I whispered.

He wrapped his arms around my torso and squeezed until our bodies merged into one. A singular, fucked-up entity. I pressed down on him, my body shuddering with pleasure. He groaned against my neck as I tightened around him.

"I want you to fuck me," I pleaded as the waves of my orgasm faded.

The timer sounded, and his inhibitions disappeared into the fabric beneath him. Despite the risk, I released my hold on his proverbial leash, letting him take me the way he wanted. He looked down at me with fire in his eyes as he lifted me up and laid me down on the couch. His rough kisses landed on my mouth before trailing down to my chest. He bit at the soft flesh of my breasts. My whimpers only made him harder.

His hands were on either side of my head. I wrapped my arms around his, and my fingers grazed his scars. They were almost identical to mine. I took a sharp breath and raked my nails over them. I looked into his eyes and tried to imagine him as Dylan, not Benjamin. The scars marked the wrong body.

When the look in his eyes shifted, I was no longer afraid. I touched his chest, grazing more scar tissue. He grabbed my wrists in one hand and pinned them above my head. His other hand raced down my side before grabbing my hip. I was his to take. There was no stopping him, and I didn't want to.

Benjamin pressed inside me and growled into the crook of my neck. The full extent of his power and passion filled me. The helpless feelings had been shed with my gown, left crumpled on the floor. The rough, hungry thrusts were everything I imagined. What I didn't expect was the way he held himself back, knowing just how much he could hurt me with his cock. I melted beneath him. I let him have my vulnerability.

I gasped as his thrusts sent ripples through my veins. "Benjamin!" I cried out. Pleasure ripped through me.

"God, you feel incredible," he murmured against the skin of my chest. "I wish I hadn't waited so long to feel you around me."

"It wouldn't have been like this if you hadn't," I said.

His powerful thrusts helped me understand the damage he could do. Possibly without even trying. My pelvis was already sore, and he was just getting started. His free hand crawled up from my hip and wrapped around my throat. My muscles instinctively tensed. Was that when his switch would flip and Benjamin would want to harm me instead of please me? He squeezed. His hand trembled with restraint. I bit my lip as a disorienting heaviness washed over me. As soon as he released, the blood flowed back into my arteries.

"Fuck," I whispered as the rush faded.

"Stand up," he commanded.

I obeyed. He leaned me over the arm of the couch with my chest pressed against the fabric. He raked his fingers over my hips and ass. They continued trailing down, and his fingers pushed inside me again. He spread my legs further with his knee and fucked me with his fingers. I glanced back at him as he pulled out and lifted his fingers to his mouth, tasting me. He growled and dropped his head back. Like a hound getting a whiff of a scent, he was locked on to me. I was his prey as well as his charge. And he was an unlikely guardian.

BENJAMIN

"I DON'T THINK I can go much longer," she whispered.

Being inside her was like the devil making love to God's sweet angel in front of him. It wasn't what I thought it would be. I thought it would be nothing—a goal post that kept moving farther and farther away. She was a challenge, and I wanted to conquer her. But the moment I sank inside her, I knew she wasn't the goal post. She was the whole goddamn game. I wanted to please her. I never gave a shit about making someone else come, but she was different.

I reached down, grabbed a fistful of her hair, and lifted her chest until she was nearly standing. I leaned close to her ear with her hair still balled in my fist. Her voice quivered and her vulnerability drove me crazy. Like the moment a serial killer tastes the blood of his victim.

"I don't want to hurt you, but knowing I am drives me harder. I want you to feel all of it. Pleasure and pain." I panted against her skin. I expected her to pull away from me —to recoil from my sick words—but she melted into the arm of the couch.

My thoughts wandered to a place where my pleasure mixed with my pain as well. The sheer pleasure of Mackenzie's body and the unbearable pain I carried from the bodies before her. I trembled at her willingness to give herself to me, without feelings of pity or resentment. My heartbeat drummed in my ears, reminding me I was alive and in the moment. Balls deep inside my little mouse, and she was everything I dreamed of.

Her moans fueled the pleasure within me and ignited a dangerous blaze in my gut. My feelings for Marcy lessened with every thrust. Marcy kept her claws in my heart, though. I'd never get rid of her, even as Mackenzie's moans penetrated my soul.

I buried my face into the nape of her neck and breathed deeply, taking in her scent and imprinting it into my memory. To relive the view, her scent, and these feelings when I was alone with Marcy. I wouldn't have a problem getting hard with that imagery, even with growing animosity toward her. She didn't know it yet, but Mackenzie's body was saving both of our lives.

My thrusts slowed as pleasure overflowed and spilled inside Mackenzie. I leaned into her, pressing my chest against her back. I released my grasp on her hair, pulled out, and turned her around to face me. She looked up at me with a single tear clinging to her lower lashes. It broke my heart as much as it made me want to show her real tears.

I put my finger under her chin and lifted it toward me. "I have never fucked anyone the way I have you."

It was true. I hadn't. Not Marcy or any of the other girls. I never gave a shit about their pleasure, focusing on their pain instead.

I leaned down and kissed her lips with a tenderness I hoped would soothe the pain between her legs. Like a wave washing away a message written in the sand. She wrapped her arms around me and relaxed against my chest. Her soft cheeks comforted the rough scars that plagued my skin.

"That was incredible," she said, her breath still laced with pleasure.

"Are you just telling me that so I don't kill you?" I pulled away and smirked at her.

"Do I have to worry about that?" She cocked an eyebrow at me.

I took a deep breath and gave her a final squeeze.

I lay down on the couch and motioned for her. Cuddling wasn't a *thing* there—Marcy thought affection was weakness—but it was a feeling I wanted to experience. She lay down in front of me, facing away from me. I wrapped my arm around her waist and pulled her into me. The warm skin of her ass pressed against me, nearly hardening me again.

I took a deep breath that relaxed my entire body. I felt calm for the first time since the night Della and I walked through that door. The feelings of warmth Mackenzie brought out of me were dangerous and deadly, but I didn't care at that moment. Tomorrow? That would be another story.

Chapter Sixteen

MACKENZIE

We woke up wrapped in each other's arms. The potent scent of sex had dissipated. He stirred beside me, his hand instinctively going to my hip.

"Morning," I whispered as I stretched, trying to rid my body of sleep.

"I can't believe we fell asleep like this. If Marcy came home last night or this morning, we would have ended up with a bullet in our heads."

"Well, thank god she didn't, I guess." I wiped the sleep from my eyes. What did he want me to say? A bullet on the couch was better than a bullet in the basement.

"We're being real fucking reckless," he said with a frustrated shake of his head. "I wouldn't have risked this before." He took a sharp breath. "Well, before you."

I lifted a curious eyebrow. "You never brought anyone else upstairs on your own?"

He shook his head. "Never. I wouldn't have. They only came upstairs for showers and for the bedroom."

"Can we go in there?"

"Into the bedroom?" He cocked his head.

"Yes." I raked my fingernails over my thigh, trying to numb my nerves. I needed to see the room—to look at it with eyes not glossed over with fear. The ducks. The snow globes. The dingy, sunken mattress. I wanted to view these things without the fog of panic and show myself I had nothing to be afraid of.

He stared at me, trying to understand why I'd have a desire to go into that room. I couldn't articulate my needs into words. Instead, I stood up and headed toward the bedroom without him. With no choice, he followed me.

"Mouse, wait!" he yelled toward me, but I was already in the doorway.

I took a few steps forward, slow and calculated like a wary animal. I ran my hand along the rusted metal headboard. My fingers traced the crackling paint behind it. I lay on the mattress with my legs pressed tightly together, my nude body small and vulnerable.

"I was so scared that day," I whispered as I looked up at the ceiling.

Benjamin came into the room and sat at the end of the bed. He'd slipped his boxers on, and his hardness tented the thin fabric.

"Are you thinking about me or them?" I gestured toward his lap.

"You don't want to know what I'm thinking about," he said with a shake of his head.

"Tell me." I didn't look at him as I spoke.

"No," he said. "You would *not* handle it well."

I scoffed. "Try me."

He hesitated until I could almost hear the slight pulse of his heartbeat as it grew faster. When he finally spoke, his voice startled me. "Well, if you insist." He stood up and crawled over me, pinning my legs beneath him. He touched my cheek. "I was thinking of you in that vulnerable position that day. Your legs spread. You begged. I had such a hunger for you. I didn't give a fuck about your feelings or the pain I would cause you." He leaned down and bit my collarbone. "I wanted to take you, and as incredible as last night was, I still fantasize about you fighting beneath me." He growled against the skin of my chest.

I couldn't believe what I was hearing. He still wanted to take me against my will, even after I gave myself so openly. A contrasting feeling tickled between my legs. "Benjamin," I said.

He stared at me. "See, I told you. I can't help what I am."

"If that's how you feel, I can't say or do anything to change that."

He slid his hand behind my neck and drew my face close to his. He pressed his lips to mine, and instead of denying him, I opened my mouth and let him in again.

"I don't want to hurt you. I don't know why this other side of me does," he whispered against my mouth.

"Come here," I whispered as I motioned next to me in bed.

He rolled onto his side. "What?" he asked as he pulled me into him.

"I need you to tell me about that girl we had to bury."

"I already told you how she died." He blew out a breath.

"I know. I want to know how she lived."

He hesitated for a moment before speaking. "Her name was Samantha. Marcy found her hitchhiking on the thruway. She starved herself to—"

"No, Marcy killed her," I corrected.

"Marcy killed her because she was starving herself. I tried everything to get her to eat."

"Was she beautiful?" I asked as I shifted my weight to look at him.

Benjamin closed his eyes. "Almost too beautiful to exist. And she ended up being just that."

"Did you rape her?"

"Over the course of the three months she was with us, yes. A lot. Marcy knew what was coming and wanted to get as much use out of her as she could."

"You raped her even as she was starving to death?" I couldn't hide my shock. Each time I thought I'd seen his lowest low, I discovered another floor beneath it.

"I had to. You know this." He avoided my gaze.

"You *had* to fuck someone who was near death?"

"Mouse," he whispered.

I turned my face away, unwilling to acknowledge him.

"I'm sorry."

"I'm not the one you need to apologize to," I snapped.

He put a little distance between us, interlaced his hands over his bare stomach, and looked up at the ceiling. A rickety old fan turned above us. It let out a squeaky whine, keeping time with my heartbeat in my ears.

"Do you regret sleeping with me?" he asked.

I turned my head to look at him. "I don't regret it, but I'm disgusted."

"I regret it."

BENJAMIN

SHE LIFTED herself onto her elbows. "What?"

"I regret it because you aren't different now. You're just

another woman who was underneath me." My words were ice, freezing her in front of me. "I shouldn't have slept with you."

She blinked several times, her lips drawn in a tight line. "You really believe that?"

I narrowed my eyes. "That's why my desire to take you against your will is so strong. You're just like the others."

I'd betrayed whatever relationship she thought we had, and she was breaking in front of me. That was fine. She needed to hate me. The more distance I could put between us, the better. What we'd done could never leave that room. Just one more secret to add to the pile of haunted and stolen dignities. We'd only be more than what we were in her imagination. And mine.

She climbed out of bed and stormed off without another word, unwilling to vomit more hatred onto my lap. I deserved that. If she fell for me, she was dead. If I fell for her, we were both dead. Despite that, I couldn't help but push into her pussy—the goddamn holiest of grails.

Forgive me, for I have sinned. And I fucking loved it.

MACKENZIE and I sat at the table together. She picked up the fork and moved it around her plate, pushing food back and forth.

"Will you please eat?" I put a forkful of scrambled eggs into my mouth. They were dry and stiff, but still edible.

"I'm not hungry," she said, still swirling her fork. The scrape of metal against ceramic grated my nerves.

I dropped my fork and looked at her. "Can you stop being upset with me?"

I needed her to hate me, but I didn't *want* her to. If I

couldn't keep distance between us, I'd be punished for my impure feelings for our captive. Marcy would kill her and make me watch. Once she'd thoroughly ripped my heart out and stomped it on the concrete floor, she'd put a bullet through my head. Or worse . . . she'd make me live with the torment.

Mackenzie was the closest thing to love I'd ever held in my hands, and I wasn't ready to let her go. With my resolve weakening, the charade was useless to try to keep up. Fuck the consequences.

"I didn't mean what I said."

"Which part?" She responded with a frostbitten tongue, and I was the one who froze her.

I wiped my mouth. "That I regretted it."

She kept her gaze locked on the light-yellow eggs. "You don't get it! I'm upset that you couldn't differentiate between what we did and what you've done with the other girls."

I stared at her, unable to do anything besides blink. I hadn't meant what I said. I could differentiate between Mackenzie and the others. I had hurt her by ripping away how special she was to me. It was my intention to push her away, but I hadn't expected her to take my heart with her. Every time I forced myself inside a woman, a little piece of my heart remained within them, but when Mackenzie allowed me inside, she took the whole damn thing.

"Come with me," I commanded. When she didn't move, I grabbed her hand, led her toward the bedroom, and pushed her into the room.

Her body trembled like leaves during a storm. "Benjamin, what're you doing?" she asked with a clenched jaw. She was afraid of me again.

I pushed her onto the bed, forcing her legs apart as I leaned over her. Instead of making me soft, her doe-eyed look hardened me. My body was so goddamn confused. Or maybe it was my mind. One wasn't talking to the other.

"You know what I want to do." I growled and lowered the waistband of my boxers, letting my cock fall from the fabric. "There's only one thing I'm thinking about right now." I rubbed my hand down her stomach and palmed her pussy.

She tensed and tried to pull away from me, but I grabbed her hands and pinned them at her sides. She was immobile beneath my weight. She looked terrified, as if I hadn't made her come the night before.

"Benjamin, stop!" she whimpered as tears filled her eyes.

"You know pleading turns me on more," I whispered. I pressed myself against her with no fabric between us.

The heat of her against my skin tempted me to burn her in return. A tear overflowed and rolled down her cheek. I slapped the nose of the beast inside me, banishing him for the moment. I leaned down and kissed Mackenzie's neck as she writhed against my grasp. I reached up and kissed her protesting lips.

"What the *fuck?*" she screamed.

A smile crept across my face. "I just wanted to show you."

"Show me what?"

"That you're different," I whispered. "I wouldn't have stopped if I saw you like I saw the other women." I stood and pulled up my boxers.

It was true. Once I got to that point, nothing could stop me. Like a dog trained to fight, I would attack until the thing between my teeth stopped squirming. But for her, I let go. That was the best way I could show her, as disgusting as it was.

"That was the dumbest, most fucked-up way to prove that point!" She sat up and pulled her gown down to cover the exposed flesh.

I stared at her with a grin, more proud of myself than anything. "How else could I have shown you?"

"I don't know, with your words maybe?" She stared back at me, shooting daggers from her eyes.

"I needed to *show* you how different you are, not just tell you," I whispered. I looked down at my hands as I sat beside her. Even once I reached the point of throbbing desire for her, I controlled myself. Her intoxicating pleas fell on ears newly deaf to the sound. Maybe not deaf. The sounds still reached me, but the feelings they evoked were muted and small.

"I'm sorry," I said with a shrug.

She blew hair off her forehead.

"Come here." I motioned her toward me.

She didn't move for a moment. She stared at the hem of the gown, her fingers plucking a loose thread. Finally, she let out a sigh and crawled toward the head of the bed. She was still pissed off—her body still flushed with the color of frustration—but it was hard to stay mad when we had so little time left.

Drawn to me like a satellite crashing toward Earth, she nestled under my arm and rested her head against my bare chest. The creases of her eyes were still wet from tears. I leaned into her and kissed her head, wrapping her up in my arms. Even knowing the interaction could get us killed, we couldn't deny the desire we'd created.

The relationship and situation were fucked up. I was poor company, but she'd forgive me because I was all she had, and she'd remain the embodiment of a life I longed for, whether she forgave me or not.

"What are these from?" She pointed to long, thin scars along my belly.

"A whip," I said. The lashing sounds echoed in my head, years after the final crack of the leather.

"A whip?" Her jaw went lax.

"Yes. Benjamin would whip me until I was cut open and bleeding, and then add a few more for good measure."

"Why did he hate you so much?"

"He thought Marcy would take me to bed one day, and she did." I shrugged. I wasn't in the mood for an interrogation, but I owed her a few answers.

"Did she sleep with you before Benjamin died?"

"No, but she sucked me off a few times before he did. She fucked me the first time next to Benjamin's body. She couldn't keep her eyes off him as she rode me." I remembered her reaching out to touch his ashen skin, turning his head just so she could spit on his face.

"So how the hell did it become this?"

My eyebrows lifted. Her curiosity was morbid.

"Eventually, I wasn't enough for Marcy anymore. She needed something else."

She let out a long exhale. "So she'd find you women?"

I didn't answer her. She knew the damn answer.

Mackenzie leaned up on her elbows. "She doesn't sleep with the women, so what does she get from this?"

"She enjoys the power and the control. It's like a drug to her. The longer she's addicted, the more she has to have to keep from getting sick." I sighed. "Now she's escalated to torture, and it's too fucking much."

Mackenzie leaned in and kissed me. Her lips were soft yet powerful. Almost hungry. She never acted starving, even when she was. Her hands grazed my chest before drifting down to my stomach and landing on my lap. I groaned at her firm, sure touch. The surety I had hoped for. My excitement grew and swelled beneath her hand. She crawled over my lap and straddled my waist, lifted her other leg over, and hopped onto the floor, pulling away from me with a smile.

"Hm, having the power did feel pretty good." She laughed

as she stood up and pulled down the hem of her gown. "Even if it's just for a moment."

"Damn it, mouse!" I groaned, my hand tugging at the front of my boxers. "You're so lucky I . . ." I didn't finish my thought. She was just lucky.

Chapter Seventeen

MACKENZIE

Benjamin flopped onto the couch. I followed after him and rested my head on his lap. He hardened beneath my cheek.

"Really, Benjamin?"

"Sorry," he said.

I sighed but didn't move my head from his lap, even with the temptation of him so close to my mouth. "Would you rub your hands through my hair?" I whispered.

Benjamin lifted an eyebrow. "What? Like, pet you?"

"I mean, kinda, yeah." I shrugged my shoulders before relaxing into him again.

He put an unsure hand on the side of my head and brushed through my hair with his fingertips. I groaned, and my lips slightly parted.

He curled his lip. "This is weird."

"No it's not. Watch." I sat up and switched positions with him, motioning for him to lay his head on my lap.

He unfurrowed his brow and nestled his head against my

thighs. "This isn't helping my situation, you know." He gestured toward the front of his pants.

"Stop and relax for a minute," I commanded as I brushed my hand through his long hair.

A low groan rolled past his lips. "Oh, I see what you mean." His words dripped with pleasure, and he relaxed against me.

"Do you and Marcy cuddle at all?" I asked, although I was sure I knew the answer. Marcy didn't seem like the cuddling type.

Benjamin snorted a laugh. "Oh god, no. If I asked her to, she'd shoot me on the spot. She thinks affection is for the weak."

I dropped my gaze as I continued stroking his hair. "That's really sad."

"Is it? Look how great I turned out." He laughed.

I slapped his arm. "I'm serious! Maybe if Marcy had been cuddled a day in her life, neither of us would be here."

"It would take more than a little affection to derail Marcy," Benjamin said as he grazed the inside of my thigh. My skin answered his touch by raising in goosebumps.

I covered his hand and stopped his ascent. "Hey!"

"What?"

I kept my hand over his, but I didn't push him away. His head was so close to my warmth. If he turned just a few inches to the left, his mouth . . .

"Have you ever even gone down on a woman?" A sly smirk crawled across my face.

"If you count Marcy grinding on my face, yes." Benjamin scoffed.

"First off, gross." I shivered. "Second, that doesn't count."

"I mean, it kinda does." Benjamin shrugged.

"God," I whispered.

His fingers crept further up my thighs, but I didn't stop

him. Instead, I spread my legs. With the clear invitation, he let his hand explore.

"If you're going to do it, do it right." I guided him to the floor, letting him crawl between my legs as I spread them wider.

He didn't need to be told twice, even though I expected more of a fight from him. His hand found its home between my legs again. My moans grew louder with every stroke of my clit. He pushed his fingers inside me and palmed me, and I moved my hips to rock against his hand.

"Use your tongue," I whispered.

He wrapped his hands around my thighs, pulling me toward the edge of the couch. He gripped my hips, dropped his head between my legs, and looked up at me. The wet heat of his tongue sent a shock of pleasure through my body as he licked me with unstifled passion. Tasting me. Enjoying me. His tongue flicked against my skin, and his beard tickled the awakened nerves between my legs. My moans grew louder. I grabbed a fistful of his hair, pulling him deeper into me. My thighs trembled as I grinded into his mouth.

"Don't stop!" I pleaded. I teetered on the edge of ecstasy, so close.

His wanting tongue refused to stop until I shuddered and trembled against his mouth. Once he knew I came, and the waves of pleasure broke, he peeked up from between my legs, wiping his mouth with the back of his hand. He climbed up and kissed me. My taste lingered on his lips.

"How did you do that?" I collapsed against the couch; my cheeks flushed with heat.

"Do what?" Benjamin cocked his head. "Is it so hard to believe I could get you off with my mouth?" He grinned and raised his eyebrows at me.

"Well, you've been isolated with Marcy for eleven years,

and your source for sex has been mostly non-consensual." I crossed my arms over my chest.

"Do you need to bring that up when I can still taste you on my tongue?"

"I'm just saying, the odds were stacked against you." I smiled and flashed my blue eyes toward him.

The crunch of gravel beneath tires wiped the smile from my face. Our eyes flew to the door. He rushed to the window and peeked through the curtain. I stayed on the couch, too frozen with panic to do much more than breathe, and even that was a struggle. His shoulders relaxed, and he let out the breath he'd been holding.

"Just a car making a U-turn in the driveway," he said. Sweat beaded along his brow. "Fuck, that was close."

He walked back toward the couch and looked down at me. His lips formed a deep frown. I knew what it meant. Marcy could come home at any moment, and it was time for our tryst to end. If that had been Marcy's car, we'd have been in deep shit. The *deepest* of shit.

"Do what you have to do," I whispered, dropping my head. I didn't want to go back to the basement, solitary and stinking. I wanted to stay upstairs and continue playing this fucked-up game of house.

We walked toward the basement, our steps slow and intentionally drawn out. We wanted to hold on to that moment for as long as possible. Every step forward brought me closer to captivity once again.

"I'm sorry I have to do this," he said as he clamped the cold manacle around my slender wrist. The sound of the lock echoed in the small basement.

I shook my arm. The chains rattled their metallic response. "I know," I mumbled. I understood his need to lock me up, even if I wasn't happy about it.

"I just don't know when Marcy will be home." The words came out in a flood, and his gaze shot toward the stairs.

"I know."

He sat down beside me and stretched his legs in front of him. He reached out and grabbed my hand, and I gave it a reassuring squeeze. The roles were reversed. I was the one chained to a concrete wall. He had the freedom to walk around the house, eat normal food, and piss in a toilet instead of a bucket, yet he needed comforting more than I did. The clammy feel of his sweat-slicked palm told me that much.

He leaned over and brushed the hair out of my face. He touched his lips to mine. We stayed with our foreheads together, motionless, as if saying a final goodbye to my freedom. Or each other. When Marcy returned, our time together would become a hazy memory. Maybe that was for the best.

"If Marcy asks, the basement flooded and I had to unlock you and put you in one of her old gowns," he said as he withdrew from me.

"There's not even any water down here." I motioned toward the dry basement floor.

He nodded, got to his feet, and walked upstairs, coming back down carrying a five-gallon bucket. Water sloshed with every step. He placed the bucket down, and more water cascaded over the sides. He wiped sweat from his forehead, lifted the bucket again, and tipped it on its side. Water rushed across the concrete and slithered toward me, soaking the bottom of my gown before I could even stand up. The cold sank through to my skin.

"Fantastic," I mumbled. I held the fabric away from me.

"Sorry," he said with a shrug of his shoulders.

"It's fine. It's believable now, if nothing else."

Benjamin froze and looked at me with wild eyes. At first, I wasn't sure what had him so afraid. Then I heard it. A rattling sound from upstairs. The distant jingle of keys. Footsteps. We held our breath, every muscle in our bodies tensed with anticipation, like two mice about to be spotted by a house cat. Had Benjamin waited even a minute longer to usher me downstairs, we'd have been torn to shreds by her angry claws.

"Benjamin?" she yelled.

"I'm in the basement!" Benjamin called back.

Her footsteps grew closer until they creaked along the rickety stairs.

"What the hell are you—" Her sentence cut off as she saw the water in the basement. "What happened?" Her mouth dropped open, exposing her yellowing, gapped teeth.

"The basement flooded." He picked up and shook the bucket as if he'd been removing the water by hand instead of placing it there to begin with.

She looked at him and narrowed her eyes. When she turned her attention to me, I fought back the urge to swallow. She'd see the bob in my throat and realize my fear. I screamed at my lungs to go at an even pace while they screamed back that they needed more air.

"Why is she wearing my gown?" Her teeth came together with a click, her jaw muscles working in time with her growing suspicion.

"Her other gown got soaked. I found her in, like, three inches of water yesterday. I bailed all the water I could, and this is what's left." He held out his arm, trying to pull her attention away from me and onto the floor.

It didn't work.

Marcy sucked her teeth and walked toward me, her shoes squishing through the watery remnants. She lifted a lock of my hair and scoffed. "I guess the water cleaned her hair too?" She inhaled. "Huh, interesting."

"She was chilled to the bone. I let her shower. What if—"

"You *let* her?" She stomped toward him and pushed a finger into his chest. "What if she escaped? What if she hurt you? Then what?"

"She didn't." Benjamin held Marcy's gaze. "Besides, you know neither one of us can escape."

Marcy drew back her arm and slapped Benjamin across the face. The sound echoed in the dark room.

Benjamin placed a hand over his reddening cheek, a low growl in his throat. "What the fuck was that for?"

"For even *thinking* about an escape. After everything I've done for you!" Marcy's lips wavered between a grimace and a frown.

"I didn't say I wanted to escape. I was just saying that if I can't escape, neither can she." Talk about being reckless. He was taunting the demon.

She turned her attention back to me. "You think you can play with his head, don't you?" Her face twisted into something unrecognizable. "You think you can manipulate him?"

I opened my mouth but caught a glimpse of Benjamin behind Marcy. He gave his head an almost imperceptible shake, but it was enough to remind me of how much we had at stake if I couldn't keep my smart mouth shut.

I bit my lip, trying to rein in my attitude. "I'm sorry. I don't want to manipulate him. I'm not trying to."

"You have since I brought you here. You need to quit thinking you're worth something to either of us. I can have you replaced in a week!" Spit flew from her mouth.

I couldn't do it. If the bitch was going to kill me, I at least wanted to have my say. "Then why don't you?"

Benjamin threw his hands up behind Marcy. His shoulders dropped. He'd tried to shut me up and failed.

Marcy leaned so close that I could feel the heat of her breath against my mouth. "Things are going to get *real* ugly for you, dear. There's no point in keeping you. Neither of us can enjoy your company, you rotten little *bitch!*"

Marcy swung around and grabbed Benjamin by the arm, yanking him upstairs. Silence followed the click of the basement door—an ominous reminder of my captivity. I looked at my hands, rubbing a finger on my palm. I traced the braille of my skin—a haunting retelling.

I sat on the wet floor and drew my legs toward me. I shivered as the moisture permeated the air, making it light and chilly. Memories of Benjamin's touch gave me a warm embrace, and I sighed, longing to feel him beside me again. The ache left by his fingers was a ghostly reminder of the happiness I found, even if it had only been for a few days.

I hated myself for finding happiness in his touch. It was wrong on so many levels and tested the foundation of my dignity. Who would want to be touched by a man who so wantonly acted on his darkest desires? I felt dirty. Maybe even crazy.

I can't do this. But I wanted to.

"What's going to happen to me?" I whispered.

Chapter Eighteen

MACKENZIE

My eyes struggled to adjust to the darkness after having been allowed to go upstairs. The acrid smell of urine and sweat permeated the air around me once again. The brief moment of freedom gave me a longing I let go of while in the basement. I forgot what it tasted like until I had a taste of him. I resigned myself to my fate, whether it involved being trapped in the basement or buried in the ground beneath the large oak tree. I became lost in the thought of the freedom death would provide—the fresh air, waving branches of the trees, and cold dirt around me.

The locks rattled on the basement door, snapping me back into a reality that made death a more desirable escape. Light filtered through the open doorway and filled the basement. Benjamin came toward me with a plate in his hand, but Marcy followed close behind him, squelching my excitement at seeing him.

"Put the plate on the table. I haven't decided if I want her to have it yet," Marcy said with an uncomfortable calmness in her voice.

Benjamin set the plate down and turned toward Marcy. She lit a few candles and put them down on the table. The sight of the flames made my hands ache. Marcy walked over and circled me like a vulture assessing a kill. She pulled out a pair of large metal scissors, reached down, and roughly grabbed my face in her other hand.

"What are you doing, Marcy?" Benjamin asked.

"Oh, I'm not doing anything." She let go of my face, stood upright, and cocked her pistol. "You are, Benjamin."

"I'm not doing anything." He crossed his arms over his chest.

"You will, or I'll paint that wall behind you with your brains." Marcy flicked the barrel of the gun toward the ceiling and pulled the trigger. A beam of light reached through the newly formed hole and spread in a small circle on the floor.

"What the fuck?" Benjamin pressed his hands to his ears. "Are you crazy, Marcy?"

My ears pulsed and rang. I moved my jaw from side to side, trying to ease the sharp pain.

Marcy strolled toward him and lifted his chin with the barrel. "What did you call me?"

"Nothing." He lowered his hands and his gaze, his confidence sapped. The glow of rage in her eyes commanded him more than her words. He'd seen that look too many times before.

"Didn't think so." She pushed the pair of scissors into his hand. "Go cut her hair."

"Her hair?" He cocked his head. "Why?" His fingers grazed the metal as he took the scissors from her.

"She needs to be taken down a notch. Several of them."

She took a few steps back and aimed the pistol at Benjamin. "Now, Benjamin!"

With every step he took toward me, my eyes widened. "Benjamin, please don't," I pleaded—almost more than I had when they burned and beat me.

I already felt so ugly. He might as well jam the scissors through my heart and twist them. My body had become nothing more than a battered vessel for pain and torture. Scars and marks from my captivity replaced my soft, pure skin. My hair was a stupid thing to hold on to, but at least I still had something I could twist between my fingers to remind me of my old life. It was the last recognizable thing about me. Hair didn't wither away from lack of food. At least, it hadn't yet.

He leaned over me and lifted a chunk of my hair. *It will be okay,* he mouthed. He placed the hair between the metal and brought the blades together with a sharp *swish*. He repeated the motions as blond hair tumbled to the floor in chunks. Not wanting to give Marcy the satisfaction of my torment, I held in my tears for as long as I could. With every snip of the scissors, the sobs built in my chest until I couldn't hold them back. Finally, I wept. Burning my hands physically hurt me, but cutting my hair was a dehumanizing act. It made me feel like less of a woman.

He continued until Marcy said to stop, leaving me with uneven sprigs of short hair, nearly to my scalp in some areas. Benjamin dropped the scissors. The loud metallic *clack* echoed along the walls.

"See? She looks so much better now!" Marcy walked over and grabbed my face in her hands. She tilted her head forward and backward, trying to peer at it properly, and a childish giggle sprang from her throat. "Yes, it's perfect."

"Fuck you," I mumbled.

"What did you say, dear? I didn't hear you." Marcy leaned over and put her cupped her hand beside her ear.

"Fuck you!" This time, I yelled it. The sound emanated from deep within my gut.

Benjamin's mouth fell open. He could only protect me up to a point.

"I'm not getting involved," he said as he turned to go upstairs. "This is a fucking mess."

BENJAMIN

"BENJAMIN! STOP RIGHT THERE!" Marcy screamed.

I stopped. Her words still held power over me, whether I liked it or not.

She raised the pistol and aimed the barrel at Mackenzie's head. "Come here. Now!"

I looked back at Mackenzie, and her shoulders dropped in defeat. *All I asked was for her to watch her mouth. I can't stop the wolf when I'm not in the pack anymore.*

"No, Benjamin!" Mackenzie yelled.

I eased toward her with slow steps. Marcy responded by ramming the butt of the pistol against Mackenzie's head. Mackenzie curled up on the ground, whimpering as she held a hand to the goose egg forming against her skull.

"Pick up the scissors," Marcy commanded me.

I hesitated too long, and Marcy drew the barrel closer to Mackenzie's head. She flinched as the cold metal touched her flesh. I sighed. Mackenzie's mouth left me with no choice. I did as I was told and picked up the scissors.

"Good boy. Now cut her face." Marcy popped out her hip, a sinister smile on her face.

I shook my head. "I'm not doing that."

"Cut her cheek or she dies. Your choice." Marcy wiggled the pistol between us, the barrel aiming indiscriminately.

I caught Mackenzie's gaze. She looked up at me with eyes brimming with tears. Her lower lip trembled.

"Just do it," she whispered as she clenched her jaw.

There was no point in fighting. Once Marcy had an idea, she was like an aggressive dog; she wouldn't release until it was done.

I reached down and took Mackenzie's face in my hand. *This isn't me,* I mouthed. She nodded slightly against my hand. I took the scissors and spread the blades. Marcy kept the gun trained on Mackenzie's head with an unwavering arm. She tightened her lips at my hesitation. Sucking in a breath, I cut into the pale flesh of her left cheek. I had to use more force than expected to sear into her skin with the dull blades. She winced as a thin line of blood formed.

"Harder and deeper, Benjamin!" Marcy waggled the gun, urging me on.

I steadied my hand and cut across her cheek again, deeper this time. Mackenzie's scream raised the hairs on the back of my neck. I could hear her pain between my ears, wrestling inside my head and ripping through my mind. Tears fell to the ground between us, blending with her blood.

"Again," Marcy hissed, tapping the pistol on her hand.

I cut under the first one. The thick channel filled with crimson liquid before overflowing onto her cheeks. Her screams tore into my chest and decimated my heart. Every time I cut her, I was cutting my soul. I dropped the bloodied silver blades to the ground.

"This is so fucked, Marcy!" I shouted.

"Interesting you say that now, because you didn't think that last time." Her voice dropped, becoming low and sultry.

"In fact, if I recall correctly, you even liked it. Got hard from it."

"I did not." I shook my head, though in my gut, I knew she spoke the truth.

"Yes, you most definitely did. We fucked while you still had her blood on your hands." She smiled. "How easily you've forgotten because of her." She spat her words toward Mackenzie. "She made you weak."

I shook my head and drew a quick breath. Mackenzie made me weak, but in some ways, she made me stronger.

"Oh, she has. I don't even recognize you anymore."

"You don't recognize me? I don't even know who *you* are anymore. You're careless, reckless, and—"

"It's because of *her!*" Marcy screamed, stomping her feet. "We were fine before she came into our lives!"

"I didn't ask to be here!" Mackenzie yelled as she held the skirt of her gown to her face. The blood seeped through the fabric and painted her fingertips.

God damn it, mouse.

"Shut up!" Marcy yelled. "I regret ever bringing you here. Your time is almost up!"

"Do what you have to do, Marcy. I'm out." I threw my hands up, and with heat in my eyes, I turned to walk away. Leaving would draw Marcy with me and remove my mouse from the crosshairs. I would take the fight away from Mackenzie.

The door slammed behind us, and our angry words crawled along the walls.

MACKENZIE

The shouting stopped, and silence surrounded me again. I'd just closed my eyes when a loud thud shook the floor above me. I looked up and took a deep breath as the room fell silent again. I cocked my head, listening. Could Benjamin have finally taken a stand against Marcy? Had that been the sound of her body hitting the ground?

Something heavy dragged and scraped across the upstairs floor and headed toward the basement door. The locks rattled. Marcy appeared in the doorway, her outline surrounded by the light from upstairs. Her chest heaved as she dragged Benjamin's unconscious body down the stairs, his head thumping against every riser on the way down. A sickening thud accompanied every movement.

"Marcy? What are you doing?" My mouth dropped open, and I scrambled to my feet. The chains sang their metallic song.

"Mind your business," Marcy snapped.

She dragged Benjamin across the hard concrete, her cheeks puffing as she struggled to move him. She leaned over him and panted. Gasping for air, she pulled him toward the chain on the wall across from me. She flicked sweat from her brow and clamped the chain around his wrist, locking the tail to the plate. She wiped her sweaty hands on her pants.

"He's your problem now," Marcy said flatly. Her fiery hatred burned through me.

"Wait, what? What do you mean?" My legs quivered beneath me. Understanding why Marcy did anything was hard enough, but none of this made sense.

She didn't respond. With heavy footsteps, she climbed the stairs. The doors locked, leaving the basement silent once more.

"Benjamin?" I whispered. "Wake up!" My voice grew louder when he didn't stir. I groaned.

I sat on the concrete and watched the steady rise and fall

of his chest—the only indication that he was still alive. I rested my head against the wall and closed my eyes, zoning out to the drip from a pipe above me. Fabric shuffled against the concrete. I opened my eyes as Benjamin struggled to a sitting position. He lifted his arm toward his face. The chain rattled as it dragged on the ground. His eyes widened, and his body responded in a panic familiar to me—adrenaline overriding the grogginess.

"God damn it, not again!" He snatched at the chain with both hands.

"Calm down!" I didn't feel all that sympathetic to his plight.

"No, I will *not* calm down! You have no clue how hard I worked to stay off this fucking chain!"

"Is freaking out going to take the chain away? No! It sure as shit didn't work for me!" I took a sharp breath. "Just stop!"

"I'll kill myself before I live down here again." Frustration and fear cloaked his words.

"Yeah, and how do you plan on doing that?" I cocked my head. "Please, enlighten us both."

"All the memories, mouse. They live down here as if I never left." He looked around the room like a wild animal surrounded by metal. He ripped at the chain again, but the plate didn't budge.

"Marcy's right. You have gotten weak." I smirked at him.

"You're an asshole." He flashed his dark eyes at me. "Is this really the time to joke?"

"I mean, I've been cracking jokes the whole time I've been here. Where have you been? But just a reminder, I'm not the one who made murder jokes."

He stared at me and rolled his eyes. *One time,* he mouthed.

"What are we going to do?" he whispered.

"Well, I tried to woo my captor, and it kind of worked, but

Marcy seems pretty pissed at the both of us, so I'm not sure what we're going to do now." I dropped my head back against the wall. "What happened, anyway?"

"I don't know. She made some tea, I drank it, and I woke up down here." He sighed. "And also, you didn't *woo* me."

I shrugged my shoulders. "I mean, I kind of did."

The corners of his lips lifted but refused to become a smile. "I think you've become senile down here."

"I have. Thanks for coming to my show. I'll be here all week. Every week." I chuckled to myself. "Do you think it was because you didn't want to cut me?"

He thought for a moment. "No, I don't think that was it. I don't know. She was really weird toward me this morning. Quiet. I thought she might have been planning to kill me, but unfortunately, I'm just down here again." He dropped his face into his hands.

"I'm sure we'll find out soon enough."

I tugged at the hem of my gown, coaxed it over my thighs, and lay back on the ground. The crevices in the concrete no longer bothered me. A spider crawled across the white wall, working its way toward a large web above my head. I could relate to her victims as they struggled against captivity. I turned my head to look at Benjamin. He sat tailor fashion, with his back against the wall.

"Let's play a game," I whispered.

"I don't want to play a game, mouse." He lifted his hand, dismissing my idea.

"Just play!" I whined. "I'll ask you a question, and you have to answer."

"I have no interest in this."

I shrugged my shoulders, beginning the game without him. "Favorite color?"

Benjamin rolled his eyes. "Fine. Black."

"Whose favorite color is black?" When he didn't reply, I kept going. "Okay, your turn."

"If you're going to judge my answer, I'm not going to play."

I waited.

"What'd you do for a job?" he finally asked.

"I was an advisor for a marketing company." I ran my finger along the concrete, remembering how much I cursed my job the day before I was taken. I hated the place so much, but I would have given anything to be back in my shitty cubicle, kissing the shitty ass of my shitty boss.

Benjamin raised an eyebrow. "Sounds boring."

"It was more fun than sitting in a basement, chained to a wall." I lifted my hand and jingled my chain to make my point. "What's your favorite thing about a woman?"

"Besides the obvious, probably her hair." He smirked.

"Ah." I placed my hand on my head and played with a short chunk of hair. "Oh, I see what you did there." I smirked back. "I would almost prefer the candles over this."

"Clearly. You cried less when I cut your face." Benjamin's gaze fell to the floor. "I'm sorry for that, by the way."

"I know. The pain is brief, but this hairstyle will last much longer than that." I sighed.

Benjamin's jaw worked as he ground his teeth. "Stop hiding your fear. You're acting weird."

"I'm not acting weird. For the first time, I can say these things out loud to someone instead of thinking them to myself. My ability to find humor in the darkest of situations has gotten me through a lot in life." I smiled at him, making him nervously brush his hand through his hair.

The door rattled and flew open. We sucked in a breath and held it. Marcy walked into the room and placed a laptop on the table. Candles illuminated her face and sent distorted shadows racing across her skin.

"I'm glad I have you both here for this!" She clapped her hands together.

"Where else would we be?" I muttered under my breath.

"What is this, Marcy?" Benjamin snapped.

"Oh, you'll see. Hang on." She opened the laptop and aimed the screen between us. With a sway of her hips, she leaned over the table and typed on the keyboard. She stood up and stepped aside, a sadistic laugh crawling from her throat. Her finger depressed a button on the keyboard, and a window popped onto the screen.

Sounds of passion filled the basement. Benjamin and I looked at each other with quick recognition of our moans. Our mouths fell open, eyes returning to the screen to view our naked bodies wrapped together in the throes of passion.

Marcy clenched her jaw when Benjamin uttered my name as he came. She shook her head as she watched him wrap me in his arms and hold me. In the video, Benjamin kissed me passionately. Her gaze dropped, and she slammed the lid of the laptop closed, unable to witness any more of our intimacy.

Benjamin sat up and tried to explain. "Marcy . . . I—"

"Don't! I heard the things you said about me. Me! The person who raised you!"

Benjamin rose to his feet, his hands up. "I didn't mean anything I said!"

"Yes you did! What I saw on that video was sickening. And don't think I missed you going down on her. I told you she made you weak! Crawling on your knees to her like a dog!"

"Marcy . . ." I whispered.

"Oh, I don't want to hear a single word from you, you little slut." She wiped a tear away from her cheek. "You made him love you. That's why he couldn't stay hard. Oh my god, how long has this been going on?"

"You can't make people love you, Marcy. That's the point," I said. "And we don't love each other. We're trapped in this house, we're bored, and that happened." I gestured toward the laptop.

"I'm not sure how you feel about him since you're a dirty whore, but he loves you." She turned toward Benjamin and clenched her jaw. "He cares about you so much that he's willing to throw all this away for you." She gestured upstairs and looked at me again. "Do you even know anything about this man?"

"I know enough." I matched her gaze.

"Well, did you know that he's gotten off on the blood of other girls? Their blood on his *cock!* Did he tell you that? Or how about how he strangled one of them nearly to death before shoving his dick in her throat?" She lifted her finger and pointed toward the ceiling. "How about when he fucked a dear girl while her heart barely had a beat left in it?"

"If you listened to that video, you'd have heard him tell me some of that himself. What he's done is repulsive." I glared at him before turning my attention back to Marcy. "But the common factor in every one of those assaults has been you, Marcy."

"Do you think I was there every time he raped those women?" Marcy laughed. "He's playing you, too, if you think that. He's sick! And you invited him inside you!"

"Marcy! You created me. Even if you weren't there every time, you were still there . . . every time!" He tapped on his head.

I sat back against the wall, stunned and unwilling to defend him with that new information. I released a deflated breath. I misunderstood their dynamic. I thought Marcy used him, but he acted on his own perversions as well. My stomach twisted. The thought of his cock inside me made me nauseous.

"You guys are both as good as dead!" Marcy shrieked. "I don't know when I'll do it, but until I do, I'm going to make your lives *hell!*"

She opened the laptop again, plugged it into the wall, and stood in front of the computer, exiting and opening windows until she found what she wanted. With a sinister smile, she clicked play on a video.

Oscillating tones filled the room. The smile remained planted on her face as she increased the volume.

"Oh dear, that's not enough!" she yelled over the sound. With a quick shake of her finger, she ran upstairs and grabbed a speaker. She plugged it into the laptop, amplifying the sounds to unbearable levels.

Low hums vibrated my chest, and higher tones ripped through my ears. Marcy covered her ears and left the basement, still grinning. I put my hands up to my ears as the tones changed and affected different parts of my body. Benjamin dropped his head into his hands.

"How's your sense of humor now?" he yelled.

"Fuck off!"

Chapter Nineteen

MACKENZIE

The oscillating sounds repeated for hours until we were rocking with our ears covered and our eyes squeezed shut.

"I can't fucking take it anymore!" I screamed.

"It's not the worst thing I've experienced," he yelled, his hands still pressed against his ears.

I curled into a ball on the floor, drawing my legs toward my body and retreating into myself. I tried to rationalize with my screaming brain. It begged for silence, but there was nothing I could do to appease it. Heat flooded my ears, and I checked to make sure they weren't bleeding.

It wouldn't surprise me if they were.

Benjamin rocked slowly. He hummed a tune at the top of his voice, trying to drown out the unwavering tones.

"Has this happened to you before?" I asked.

"Not to me, but she used it on someone else."

"Did they come out of it alive? Because I feel like I might combust." My voice strained to reach over the sounds.

"Yes! It's mind over matter!" Benjamin said with feigned encouragement.

"I'll let my mind know! Apparently, it didn't get the memo!"

When the sound dropped to a lower tone, we relaxed. It created an uncomfortable hum under my skin, but it was more bearable than the opposing end of the sound spectrum. When it rose, a hand reached out from the speakers and shook my eardrums violently.

The sound stopped.

Benjamin lifted his head. "Holy fuck! I can still hear it in my head! Can you?" he yelled as he wiggled his jaw.

I gasped for air and dropped my hands from my ears to lift myself up. "I don't hear it, but my eardrums physically hurt." I gave my head a shake. "I'd rather listen to that than another word about you being a rapist, though."

"Oh my god. Really? Right now?"

I shrugged. "I mean, I don't really see a better time. We're probably going to die at any moment, and my last memory of you is knowing you're a rapist instead of a victim under her control."

"You have no idea what I've been through. This isn't very fair of you." Benjamin dropped his gaze.

"Fair? Right. Please, go on. Tell me how much of a victim you were and why that makes what you've done okay," I said.

"I *was* a victim." He clenched his jaw. "I became a monster because of it."

I nodded my head. "I'd say so."

His eyes snapped back to me. "Will you stop? You've made me a better person, and I've shown you that. I'm a better man around you."

"I don't want to be the reason you're a better person. I want *you* to be the reason you're a better person. I don't want to be the person who tames a beast. I'm not your Belle!"

His voice softened. "I'm sorry for what I've done. I can't change that now."

"I know. I just wish I knew all that before we had sex."

"You did know, mouse."

My eyes widened. "Not the extent!"

"You were willing to fuck—for argument's sake—a rapist. I didn't realize there were levels to how rapey you could be before you were considered unfuckable." Benjamin brushed his hand through his hair.

"No, I was willing to fuck *you*. In that moment, you were just . . . you." My voice trembled and broke. I was trying to convince myself. I did have sex with a self-admitted rapist. I even *came* from sex with him. *Oh god.*

"I'm still just me. I'm no different from the person you had sex with that night."

We didn't hear the locks rattling as we spoke. Marcy walked in and glared at us. She tossed bruised apples toward us, unwilling to prepare anything more substantial. We didn't reach for the fruit as it rolled closer.

She looked at the laptop, drumming her fingers against the side of her arm. "When did that turn off?" she asked. She walked to the computer and started the video again. The nauseating tones filled the room. Marcy covered her ears dramatically. "Wow, that's really awful!" She laughed and scurried up the stairs, unwilling to be a victim of her own torture.

Benjamin and I recoiled as if we'd been struck, our bodies unprepared to deal with the sound again so soon.

After a moment, he leaned over, grabbed an apple, and bit into it. Some of the juice dripped down his chin. He wiped it away with the back of his hand. I shivered at the motion, remembering how he'd once wiped me off his chin.

"Must be nice!" I screamed. Despite the heartbeats in my

ears, the gnawing hunger in my stomach became too painful to ignore.

"It's not really doing much!" he yelled back. "Maybe taking the edge off a bit." He held the apple in his right hand and kept his left hand over his ear. He took a final bite and dropped the core to the ground.

I leaned forward, grabbed an apple, and stared at the bright red skin. I wiped its dirt-smudged flesh on my gown before taking a bite while covering one of my ears with my free hand like Benjamin had. I took meager mouthfuls, trying to savor the sweetness against my tongue. I groaned softly before placing the core on the ground.

"I have to piss!" he shouted

I took a deep breath as I grabbed the bucket by the handle and slid it toward him. I had to kick it the rest of the way.

He struggled to his feet and unzipped his jeans.

"Are you just going to do that right here?" I yelled over the horrifying sounds.

He looked around. "Where else would I do it?"

I glanced around the room, remembering our predicament. I would be in the same boat soon enough. "Fine," I said as I turned my head away from him.

"Jesus Christ, I can't even go with these sounds playing!" The frequency ratcheted to the higher pitch, and we shivered. He tucked himself back into his boxers and zipped his pants, sitting back down on the ground with a huff.

I lay flat on my stomach, my elbows on the ground and my hands covering my ears. When the sounds stopped again, I dropped my hands in front of me. Surviving the second round of the auditory assault left me breathless. Benjamin sat with his elbows on his knees as he held his ears, and he dropped his arms down and outward in the silence.

"Wow, that's fucking terrible," he said as he took a deep

breath. "Now I *really* need to pee." He stood and unzipped his jeans.

I looked away. The stream hit the barren bucket and produced a hollow sound. He groaned in relief and zipped up his jeans.

He cleared his throat. "Don't you need to go?"

"I would rather die than piss in front of you again," I said with a quick shake of my head.

"Oh my god, just go."

I rolled my eyes. My bladder screamed and my leg shook as I tried to hold back the flood. "Fine. Turn around!"

He slid the bucket toward me with his foot before turning toward the wall. The contents sloshed inside. With hesitation, I stood, lifted my gown toward my hips, and hovered over the bucket, my legs trembling as I released.

"God, I want to die," I whispered as I lowered the gown.

"Don't let Marcy hear you say that."

I pushed the bucket away and sat on the ground. "Fucking Marcy," I whispered. "I don't know how you slept with that woman."

Benjamin dropped his gaze and shook his head. "I didn't have much of a choice, did I?"

"Also, did you know there was a camera up there?" How could he not have? *Did he do this on purpose?*

"Do you think I'd have done that with you if I did?"

I shrugged my shoulders. "I don't know. You guys are into some weird shit."

"The weird shit I like doesn't involve being chained to the wall." He shook his arm, rattling the metal.

"Can you imagine what she felt when she saw us fucking?" I dropped my head into my hands, feeling a minuscule pang of sympathy for the woman.

"I think it broke her heart, if I had to guess."

"But why? She didn't care when you raped the other women without her."

"They were forced. Obviously, they didn't have feelings for me, and I didn't have any for them. I also didn't verbalize how I was losing attraction to Marcy clear as day on a video either." He paused. "It could also be because I was so affectionate toward you. Lots of levels to this."

I scoffed. "You're the one who said Marcy didn't want affection, so I don't see why it matters."

"Couple all that with not staying hard enough to fuck you in front of her, and I can see why she's pissed." He brushed a hand through his hair. "Things have been uncomfortable between us since that day. She got clingy and could tell I wasn't fucking her the same way I used to. I can't just turn off my feelings and let my body do its thing anymore." He shrugged, sitting quietly for a while before continuing. His voice sounded small when he spoke, like he didn't want to ask the question, but he couldn't help himself. "Would you have had sex with me if you weren't in this situation?"

I swallowed hard. There wasn't any reason to spare his feelings, but it still pained me to tell him the truth. "No, I wouldn't have. You aren't really my type."

"What's your type? Someone who's smarter? Or doesn't look like a monster?" His words were harsh, and I could hear the hurt buried within them.

"No, not so much that. I've just never been particularly attracted to people who commit sexual assault." I shrugged and smiled.

"Can't you be serious for one minute?"

"Oh, no, I'm very serious. That's never been attractive to me." I flashed my smile at him again.

He stretched out on the ground and sighed. "I hate you."

"No you don't." I grinned, letting silence wash over us for

a few minutes before I spoke. "Would it make you feel any better to know you fucked me better than anyone has?"

Benjamin scoffed. "Guess your bar is low."

"No, it's not. It was incredible. You had such a hunger for me."

"I still do," he said as he stared at the ceiling.

I watched his chest rise and fall rhythmically. The tension under the zipper of his jeans made me bite my lip as my mind wandered to the length of him beneath the fabric. I imagined his strength behind me and inside of me. My breath grew shallow. As much as the thought made my thighs clench, it also turned my stomach. How was I still attracted to him, even after I learned the extent of his evil?

But he was right. I knew all along. When he pinned me against the wall and growled with frustration, I knew what he was capable of, and somehow, it made what we did together more confusing. And special. When a wild animal mauls everyone else and then gently licks your hand, you can't help but feel chosen.

I sighed and scooted back until I could rest my head against the wall.

"Being down here with you is almost worse," he mumbled.

I turned my head to look at him. "Why?"

"When those sounds were playing, the only thing that calmed my mind was thinking about lying with you. Whenever I look at you, all I can think about is being inside you again. Fucking you." He took a deep breath. "It was easier to ignore that ache when I was upstairs."

I looked at him. When my brain screamed, thoughts of him soothed me as well. How could I tell him his touch occupied my mind at the worst moments? Even as he cut my face, his firm grasp on my chin reminded me I was safe. In one beat of my heart, his words comforted me, but in the next, hatred for him filled me. How could I explain that when I didn't understand it myself?

When his body pressed against mine, it felt like home. And I was homesick.

Chapter Twenty

MACKENZIE

We woke to the sound of the door unlocking. I sat up and blinked until my eyes focused. Marcy walked to the table and lit a candle without a glance in our direction.

"I just have to ask, Benjamin." She turned toward him as he sat up with a yawn. "Why?"

Benjamin raised his eyebrows. "Why what?"

"Why'd you have to sleep with her? What did I do to deserve this? I've taken care of you since you were, what, fourteen? I loved you!"

"I loved you too, Marcy. If you just let me come back upstairs, I'll show you!" He stole a glance in my direction.

Marcy put a finger to her chin, contemplating his request. She sucked her teeth. "No, Benjamin. I can't ever trust you again. You betrayed me. You called me crazy!"

"I was just trying to impress her," he said in a smooth, velvet voice.

I scrunched my nose and dropped my head into my hands. His eagerness to say anything to save his own ass was a turnoff. If Marcy asked me, I would tell the truth—Benjamin fucked me like Marcy didn't matter—so I silently prayed she wouldn't ask.

"Why would you want to impress her?" Marcy asked.

Benjamin stood and walked to the end of his chain. "Because you brought her home for me, and I wanted to use her."

"Even if that was the case, why'd you stop having sex with me?" Marcy jammed her fists against her hips.

"I was just confused. She was playing mind games with me. You said it yourself. She plays games." He looked at me and spat the words, making my jaw drop. "I was stupid and let her get between us."

"Prove it to me."

She walked toward him, unbuttoning her jeans and letting them fall to the ground. Benjamin embraced her intentions and unbuttoned his fly with excited fingers. He leaned into Marcy but avoided her kiss by dropping his face into the crook of her neck. My eyes were as confused as my heart.

He pushed her against the wall, facing her away from him. Pinning her against the concrete, he pulled her panties down. He grabbed her hips, his fingers dimpling her flesh, and spat on his hand before rubbing it between her legs. He pushed inside her. Marcy let out a gasp similar to the noise I made when I felt his strength inside me. As he pounded against her ass, I stared with a disgusted curiosity. His body moved the same way it had with mine, blurring my feelings further.

Marcy moaned in time with Benjamin's short and quick thrusts, his hand reaching up to grab her neck. I hoped he would snap the vertebrae beneath his fingers and end our nightmare once and for all. Instead, he squeezed the sides of her neck and silenced her sounds of pleasure. When he released his grasp, she leaned against the wall. The same disoriented wave that had once washed over me was washing over her. I turned away and forced back tears as I realized this was all a game to him. A sick, fucked-up game.

Benjamin's thrusts slowed, and his groans bounced against the walls, multiplying the sounds. "I missed that," he said with a pleasure-laced voice.

Marcy looked back at me, her eyes playful and taunting. "See? He loves me, not you."

I didn't let my gaze land on her, unwilling to give her the satisfaction.

"She's nothing to me, Marcy. Not like you are." Benjamin groaned into her shoulder. "I wouldn't even care if you killed her."

That got my attention. I stared at the back of his head, unsure if he could feel the daggers I threw with my eyes.

"Soon," Marcy whispered.

Benjamin pulled out and zipped up his jeans. Marcy stepped into her panties and reached for her pants, staring at me with a renewed sense of power.

"Marcy, can you unlock this chain?" Benjamin asked with a rattle of the metal.

She traced her jaw with her finger, thinking over his request. "I want to, but you'll have to show me you mean it a few more times before I believe it. I don't want to watch my back in my own house, so I need to be sure." She smiled at me before walking back upstairs and locking the door on her way out.

Benjamin slid down the wall and sat on the ground, putting his head in his hands.

"Wow," I whispered.

He opened his mouth to speak.

"Don't." I lifted my hand and dismissed him, turning away from him. My heartbeat drummed in my ears—a deafening pulse in my head.

"Mouse," Benjamin said. When I didn't respond, he raised his voice. "Mouse!" He grew frustrated with my silence. "You know I had to try. It's the only chance I have to get off this chain."

"You told her to kill me. Are you fucking kidding me right now?" My words were fire, lighting the whole damn basement aflame. "I could almost understand that you might have been playing her, but I don't know. It feels like I'm the pawn. What was your plan, anyway?"

"I figured if I fucked her, she'd forgive me and let me come back upstairs," Benjamin said with a shrug.

"And?"

"Then I would work on getting you out." Benjamin kicked his feet out as he sat down.

"Then why tell her to kill me? Why plant that idea in her head? She's already itching for a reason to pull the trigger on me!"

"I don't know. Believability?"

"Exactly. You haven't changed. You just know how to put on an act for whoever you're trying to entertain in the moment. I'm disgusted." I sat on my heels.

"You have to learn how to play games to survive." He squinted. "Wait, how do I know you weren't playing games by sleeping with me? Were you doing what I did with Marcy? Earning my trust and making me fall for you to get what you want?" Benjamin's gaze shot back to me, his lips drawn tight.

"I wouldn't have shed my dignity to sleep with you like that. I would have taken my own life rather than sleep with you when I first came here. I felt the same way until one day, I didn't anymore." I sighed. "It blows my fucking mind that I'm attracted to you. I *am* going crazy down here. You've been a major source of pain for me, and for some fucked-up reason, I don't want to lose you, which is exactly what I feel like just happened."

Benjamin tugged at his chain, wrapping it around his hand. "I did it for you."

"I want to believe that, but no one is *that* good at acting. You fucked her like you fucked me."

"I fucked her like that because I was imagining it was you!" Benjamin whispered with heat on his tongue, fighting my fire with his own.

"Jesus Christ, in what realm does that make it okay?" I threw my arms up.

"This one," he said. "You're going to have to accept some fucked-up shit as being okay here, mouse."

"Nope. I won't accept that." I shook my head.

Benjamin stood and walked to the edge of his chain. "Well, you have to. Do you know how bad I want to touch your face? To kiss you again? That's not normal for me. That feeling is entirely foreign. I thought love was what I felt for Marcy, but this isn't the same. I'm down here because I risked everything to be with you for two days. We might die because I couldn't control my desire to touch you and be inside you. How do you think that makes me feel? I have to do *something,* and if that means sleeping with Marcy, I'm going to try." He sighed. "Talk about sleeping with the enemy."

Enemy? He finally realizes she's the enemy?

"I'm sorry, okay?" he said.

"I want to touch you too. I want to let you kiss me. It hurt me more than it should have to see you two. That's how I know this isn't a survival instinct type of game for me. You can get back in her graces with that bargaining chip." I pointed to his crotch. "But I'll probably die on this chain. And soon."

"I can't think about that," Benjamin said with a quick shake of his head.

"If I have to think about it, so do you. She's going to kill me, and you know that best of all. There are girls like me buried under that tree out there." I gestured toward the backyard.

"They aren't like you," Benjamin whispered.

"You're right, they aren't like me. They *were* me."

Chapter Twenty-One

BENJAMIN

Marcy appeared in the shadows, her footfalls so quiet we almost didn't hear her. She lit a candle. Her wide smile gleamed behind the flame and made me uncomfortable. She walked to Mackenzie and unlocked her chain, the metal tail dragging along the floor.

"What are you doing?" Mackenzie asked with a nervous dart of her eyes toward me.

"You look a little too cozy on the floor. I'd like to change that." Marcy tossed Mackenzie's chain over the rafter and tugged with a heaving groan. She dug her heels in and squatted to gain leverage as she lifted Mackenzie to her feet.

Mackenzie squirmed and tried to fight against the chain, her arm rising above her head. "Come on, Marcy, please!" Mackenzie begged. "This really hurts!"

"That's the point." Marcy grunted, yanking link after link toward her chest.

Mackenzie tried to make herself as heavy as possible, but her thin frame was no match for Marcy's strength. As the madwoman used the chain like a pulley, Mackenzie's body lifted until she was just able to graze the floor with the tips of her toes, her arm hyperextended.

Marcy used the lock to attach the chain to itself. The moment she released it, the chain shifted a few inches around the beam, allowing Mackenzie to drop onto flat feet before the chain hit the end of its length. She took a deep breath. The full weight of her body was off her arm, but she still couldn't lower it. She didn't understand how awful that position would feel after only an hour, but I did. I knew.

My skin crawled with memories of being hung from the rafters. The pain and hopeless exhaustion of my body. Until I couldn't do it, I never realized what a blessing it was to relax my arm at my side. As a kid, my grandpa told me stories of wild animals gnawing off their legs to escape one of his traps. I never understood his stories more than when a chain held my arm at such an unnatural angle.

Sweat beaded on my forehead and slicked the surfaces of my palms. I wiped them on my dirty jeans. My mouth drew downward as the fear squeezed my lungs.

Marcy turned toward me. "Do you have a problem with this, Benjamin?" She stepped closer, and her hot breath brushed against my cheek.

"No . . . no I don't." I stammered. "I think it's a great idea. It will definitely humble her."

"I think so too!" Marcy smiled and touched my cheek. "Let me get you food."

Mackenzie looked over at me and shook her head. Tears silently slipped past her cheeks and onto her gown, but I noticed every drop. Her extended left arm lifted her gown on that side and exposed the skin from her upper thigh to the bony knot of her hip.

Marcy walked up the stairs with a sway in her rear,

renewed excitement in her steps. She reappeared with a warm plate in her hand. She handed it to me with a smile.

"Can I have something to eat?" Mackenzie whispered.

I shivered, knowing how hard it was for Mackenzie to ask Marcy for anything.

"Oh, no, I don't think so." Marcy's smile dropped. "You don't deserve to eat." She walked back upstairs, locking the door on her way out.

Mackenzie wiggled her arm to test the chain.

"There's no point," I said. I tried everything to slip from the chain when I was hanging there. Nothing worked.

"I know it's pointless, but I have to try." Mackenzie tucked her chin against her chest and sighed. "Are you really going to keep eating while I'm stuck like this?" Her stomach let out a hungry gurgle to support what she'd said.

"I'm sorry." I dropped the plastic fork and swallowed what was already in my mouth. I put the plate down in front of me.

"What is this, Benjamin?" She motioned toward the chain with her untethered hand.

"I believe the technical term is called a stress position. That's what Benjamin used on me to gain control."

Mackenzie looked toward the rafters, her neck straining against the angle of her arm. "Do you think she's trying to gain control or kill me? Honestly?"

"I'm not sure." I didn't know what Marcy's endgame was.

Mackenzie sucked air through her nose. "That smells so good. My stomach is eating itself."

I looked down at the plate. "If I had a way to give this to you, I would."

"Bring it to the end of your chain," she said.

I grabbed the plate and stood up, extending myself as far as I could. Mackenzie twisted her body and stood on tiptoes, reaching toward me with her free arm until she could graze the white porcelain plate with shaking fingers.

"Come on!" She gritted her teeth and leaned harder against her chained arm. She ignored her pain and pushed her shoulder to the limit until I feared it would pop out of place. With a final jerk, she grabbed the plate between her finger and thumb.

"You got it?"

"I think so," she said through clenched teeth. I let go of the plate, and Mackenzie managed to keep hold of it.

"I'm sorry for what you're going to witness," she said before dropping her face onto the plate. She ate what she could without her hands, swallowing hard.

Once she was satisfied, we repeated the strained dance until I had the plate back on my side of the room. I ate what was leftover, put the plate down, and kicked it away with my foot.

I sat down and dropped my face into my hands. Seeing Mackenzie like that pained me. She became an embodiment of my torture. I knew what she was up against, but at least she had me. As sad as that was. I had been alone and exhausted, with no one to keep me company or encourage me to keep going. My legs would often give out, and I'd drop, nearly ripping my arm out of its socket. The pain was indescribable. It shocked me with adrenaline and gave me the strength to scramble to my feet again.

I didn't know how to warn her of what was to come.

MACKENZIE

"I CAN'T WATCH you like this," Benjamin said.

"Why not? I'm just standing here." I licked my dry lips. It felt like days had passed on the end of the chain, but it couldn't have been more than a few hours.

"They kept me standing like that for days at a time. After twenty-four hours, your legs don't even belong to you anymore, and it's a fight to keep them beneath you."

"You don't think she'll keep me like this for days, do you?" My words trembled.

"I'm afraid she will."

I shook my head and looked at my feet. "I don't understand what I did to deserve this."

"You didn't do anything. It's my fault. I shouldn't have slept with you." He backed up against the wall and leaned his head against the concrete. "I should've been more careful. I should've told you no when you wanted to come upstairs." His words came out in a flurry of syllables. "I was selfish."

"Do you really think this would have ended differently? Maybe not as quickly, but it was a ticking time bomb, and Marcy is the only one with access to the fuse. If she's going to kill me, neither of us can do a damn thing about it."

Benjamin lifted his head and met my eyes. "I have to do something, mouse."

"What are you going to do? Fuck for your freedom?"

"If that's what it takes."

I rolled my eyes. Jealousy eclipsed my rational side. If I'd been thinking properly, I would have encouraged him to sleep with her to get back into her good graces, but between the pins and needles in my strained arm and the selfishness in my heart, I couldn't think with my rational mind.

"What made them do this to you?" I asked. Not that they needed a reason. They did what they wanted, giving in to irrational impulses and whims faster than a toddler in a cookie factory.

"Once because I tried to get between Benjamin and my

sister. Another time for trying to escape. Oh, also when they wanted me to bury my sister and I refused."

"They wanted you to bury your own sister?"

"Benjamin was getting really sick by then. He couldn't do much anymore. He ended up making Marcy do it. He reserved his strength to hang me up for refusing." He kept his eyes away from me as he spoke.

"And you said you had to stand like this for two days?" I strained against my arm. My legs already pleaded for rest.

"Yes. The longest was three days. Marcy ended up in the hospital, and Benjamin was too drunk to remember to let me down."

"How the hell did you not give up?" I shook my head.

"You can't. Even Samantha wasn't giving up when she starved herself. She chose to go out on her terms. That girl never gave up, even though it seemed like she had."

My eyes raced along the scars on his arms. "Was she the one who scratched you?"

"Yes. If I was going to take a piece of her, she was going to make sure she took a piece of me in return. And she did." Benjamin tugged down his sleeve.

"You sound like you liked her." A hint of jealousy slipped through my defenses. *Pathetic.*

"I'm not sure about all that, but I respected her. She was a person I could have liked, yes, but I was too in love with Marcy to see past her."

"It's called Stockholm syndrome."

He cocked his eyebrow and stared at me.

"When victims form a bond with their captors," I elaborated.

For a moment, he didn't speak. "Does that mean you're Stockholmed?" He smiled.

"I guess I won't know until we get out of here." I smiled

back, trying to put it out to the universe that we would one day escape. "What made you turn on Marcy?"

Benjamin shook his head. "I never turned on her."

"Yes, you did. The moment you fucked me. When you stopped her assaults, you most certainly turned on her. Anytime you helped me, you did."

He rubbed a hand through his hair. "Even when we had no one down here, she still locked me inside, which means it was never about the women. I started to understand what I was to her, I guess."

"A pawn in her game?" I scoffed.

"Pretty much all I am." He sighed. "But I think she loves me."

"She does not," I said with a humorless laugh.

"Somewhere in her black little heart is love for me. When I couldn't, you know . . ." He gestured toward his lap. "When I couldn't do that, she shot me in the shoulder instead of the head. She's kept me alive, even when we couldn't use you as a plaything."

A plaything. I shivered at his words. That he used women as playthings in the past didn't go unnoticed, and it disgusted me. Maybe I was Stockholmed after all.

"If that's the way you measure love, you have no room to talk about my low standards." A smile tugged at the corners of my mouth.

Benjamin shrugged his shoulders. "Maybe you're right."

I dropped my head back and swayed on tired legs. My mind drifted to the woman beneath the tree. Samantha. I'd soon be joining her. And Della. And the . . . half. I snapped my attention to him. "Wait, a minute! Do you know what I just realized?"

"What?"

"We're missing a girl. You said there are *three* girls under the tree." I lifted my free hand up to begin counting on my fingers. "Your sister, Della. Samantha was another. Who's the third?"

"I'm not talking about this." He folded his arms across his chest and looked away.

"You have to."

"I don't have to. And I won't."

I stared and waited for him to cave to my questioning, like he always did. Silence drifted between us for several minutes, but finally, he spoke.

"She was here for about four and a half years."

Numb to the fuckery that happened within those walls, I didn't react to his words. "What happened to her?"

"She died." Benjamin picked at the skin around his thumbnail.

"Clearly." His avoidance made me more curious. And suspicious. "Who killed her?"

His gaze dropped to the floor, a thick silence between us.

"She did." His words were almost inaudible. "She hung herself."

I didn't ask why. Four and a half years of mental and physical abuse seemed a sufficient reason. Still, Benjamin continued and supplied me with a reason I didn't expect.

"She was pregnant with my child." His flat voice froze the blood in my veins. "I was angry at first, but then I really grew to love the idea of a baby of my own. I came down here a few days after she told me, and she was hanging from that same rafter above you."

"Why the fuck would you want to bring a baby into this life?"

Benjamin shrugged. "Something to take care of, I guess. Something Marcy could take care of. Maybe it would soften her heart."

"Get a fucking dog, not a baby."

"Marcy hates animals."

I shifted my weight, trying to relieve the pressure building in my wrist and shoulder. “Wait. How has Marcy avoided getting pregnant all this time?”

“She can’t have children.”

I stared at Benjamin and grazed my stomach with my free arm. I let him explode inside me without thought or hesitation. I wanted all of him. Every drop. I could become the next vessel for his child after our evening together. *Idiot.*

Chapter Twenty-Two

BENJAMIN

"I'm so exhausted," Mackenzie said as her head dropped forward. Her legs trembled like twigs beneath her. She switched her weight from one hip to the other, trying to give each one a brief break.

"I know how you feel," I said as I dropped my head against the concrete wall behind me.

"Do you?"

"Yes, I do. Don't take this out on me. I'm not your enemy." I knew how she felt, and seeing her that way tugged at whatever heartstrings I had left. Despite wanting to sleep with her, I'd have taken it all back—or at least fucked her in the basement—if I knew it would keep her off that rafter.

"Not my enemy *right now.* But you were definitely an enemy." She lifted her free hand toward me, showcasing the scars.

"You're sleep deprived. That's why you're projecting onto me."

"If I could project anything, it would be my fist into your

fucking throat," she croaked. She hadn't had anything to drink since getting chained to the rafter, and her throat sounded like sandpaper.

I picked at the flaking concrete by my foot. I tried to stay awake with her, but my eyelids were weighted blankets over my eyes. "I miss the comedian side of you, no matter how subpar you were at it," I whispered.

"Yeah, well, she's dead. Like my fucking arm." She tried to wiggle her raised hand. The weak movement barely shifted the chain.

"Mouse, please." I dropped my face into my hands.

I felt helpless, and it was an awful feeling. She was dying, and instead of rescuing her, I was forced to watch. For so long, I was the apex predator. Now I was the prey, stuck in a trap. Sleeping with Marcy bought us enough time to figure out a plan . . . and realize there wasn't one.

"I'm sorry," she mumbled. "I'm just so tired. Every part of my body feels like it's going to fall off or die. Maybe both."

"If I could take your place, I would." *In a heartbeat. I should be on that chain. A monster like me should be chained up. Not the sweet little mouse.*

"Yeah, yeah."

"No, I'm serious. I'm the one who deserves it," I said as I rose to my feet. "I know you can handle this, though. You can't see it, but you're strong."

I hoped my words of encouragement would speak to her trembling nerves and aching muscles, soothing them enough to keep her on her feet. Tears dropped to the floor beneath her and splattered on the concrete. Her arm strained against the weight.

"I'm tired, Benjamin. I just don't want to do this anymore."

"Don't say that. I need you."

"You don't need me. Marcy's just going to kill me, and you'll end up with someone new."

I did need her. Once I had a taste of her, being without her wasn't an option. I would chew my arm off if I had to, but I wouldn't let her die. Not since she showed me what it was like to live.

"I don't want anyone else," I said with a shake of my head. No one would ever come close to her. They wouldn't hold a candle to her. *Oh, the irony.*

"You have to face it because it's going to happen soon." Her weak voice barely reached my ears. "And at this point, I welcome it."

I fought back the teasing heat behind my eyes, the pain and the fear all too real for me. Watching Mackenzie brought back haunting memories of my abuse in the drafty basement. The feelings of hopelessness and seeking out a way to end the suffering, even if it meant ending my life.

I walked over to the wall and slid to the floor, my stomach growling and twisting on the way to the ground. *Where the fuck is Marcy?* I looked at Mackenzie's thin frame and jutting hip bones; she wouldn't survive another couple days like that.

Footsteps drew near the door, and the locks clicked apart.

Finally.

Like a skulking cat, Marcy drifted through the shadows. She approached Mackenzie and lifted her weary head with her hand. "How're you doing?" Marcy said.

Mackenzie didn't respond. It wasn't like her to keep quiet like that, and her silence scared me.

I rose to my feet. "I think she's had enough, Marcy. She's going to die if you keep her like this."

Marcy twisted her head toward me. I stepped back, cursing under my breath at my inability to stand up to her.

Her claws still dug into my mind, even after I'd removed them from my heart.

"That's the point. If she's not dead by tonight on her own, I'll take care of her." She flicked the hem of her jacket aside. The candlelight gleamed along the butt of the gun.

I cleared my throat and spoke with feigned confidence. "I mean, if that's what you want to do. I don't care." *Fuck.* I was trying every trick—throwing everything at the damn wall and hoping something would stick.

Marcy touched my face. "Maybe it should just be us for a while after she's gone. What do you think?"

She smiled and leaned in to kiss me. Her lips were like strips of dry leather. How had I ever enjoyed the feel of them against mine? My stomach tossed, and I fought back a gag as her tongue wiggled inside my mouth. Her hands wandered down my chest and slipped past the waistband of my pants. My cock lay limp and fat in her cold hand.

She pulled back. "What's the matter?" She tugged me forward by my waistband, her other hand still trying to force blood into my veins.

I grabbed her wrist. "I'm just not in the mood, alright?"

Marcy dropped her jaw, her eyebrows furrowing in suspicion. "Why not?"

"I'm starving, this basement smells like piss, and I haven't had a shower in days. If you want sex, take me upstairs. I can't do this down here."

It worked. A smile slipped across her face as she pulled the key from her pocket. With the cold metal of my freedom still in her hand, she stopped and stared at me, her eyes squinting. "Maybe this isn't the best idea right now. Not until after tonight." She motioned toward Mackenzie and looked at her watch, checking the time on Mackenzie's death clock.

So goddamn close.

I dropped my voice to a husky whisper. "I really want you, Marcy. Let me fuck you." I needed her to feel the desire I didn't have. If I had to fuck for my freedom, I would. And I'd do it for Mackenzie's as well.

"I don't trust you until she's gone. She's too manipulative!" Marcy said with a wave of her hand.

"She can't even speak. She hasn't made a sound for hours. How can she manipulate me when she's nearly dead?" I licked my lips and changed gears. "I want to be with you. I've never betrayed your trust in eleven years."

"Yes you have! You fucked her!"

"I let myself think with my cock for one night, Marcy. I snuck off to fuck the other girls when you weren't there. How is this any different?"

"There's plenty of difference in that. You kissed her. You held her. You mocked me *with* her."

I shook my head. She was right. We had acted differently. We acted like we weren't trapped—that it wasn't a relationship of convenience. We acted like we were in love.

"I heard everything," she said. "Those other women despised you. You were the thing of their nightmares. Not for her. She likes you. How could I ever compete with that?" She pointed at Mackenzie's skeletal frame, her voice breaking as she held back tears. Her momentary lapse didn't last long. She sucked in a breath and steadied her features. "I'm tired, Benjamin. I don't want to do this anymore. I love you, and when she's gone, you'll love me again."

I met her gaze, my posture rising taller. "Do you love me, or do you fear being alone?"

She paced the floor. "No, I know I love you. I should have killed you in the bedroom when you couldn't hide your feelings for her, but I didn't. You were willing to die to preserve her innocence. Why?" She stopped in front of the table and placed her palms against the wooden surface.

I needed to do something to convince Marcy I still had feelings for her. She needed to believe I wanted her, even though the thought of ramming my cock inside her sent my balls scrambling into my stomach. I looked at Mackenzie, my eyes resting on the tempting shadow of her pussy just beneath her gown. My imagination wandered to kissing up her thighs. I imagined her warmth and tightness around me. The memory made me hard. Being inside her was the closest I'd ever gotten to Heaven.

"You needed me. That's why you didn't kill me."

"It would take two bullets to get rid of her *and* you. I don't *need* you." Her lip trembled. "I don't need anyone!"

"Well, I need you!" I unzipped my jeans and put my hand down my pants. I wrapped my hand around my cock, replaying the memory of fucking Mackenzie through my mind. It was the only way I could stay hard.

Marcy's eyes widened. She walked over and wrapped her hand around me. I tried to relax my posture.

"Oh, Benjamin." She sighed. "I want to, but you'll have to wait." She ran a cold finger along my cheek and turned for the stairs. "I don't trust you yet. Once she's gone . . ." Her voice trailed away.

"Marcy!" I yelled as she continued to walk toward the door. "Can I at least have some food?"

The door slammed shut, suffocating me with the following silence.

"I was so close. Fuck." I took a heavy breath and walked toward the end of my chain, tucking myself back into my boxers. "Mouse," I whispered. "Mackenzie!" I raised my voice while clenching my jaw to stifle my tone. "You have to wake up!"

Mackenzie lifted her head. Sunken eyes stared back at me.

"She's going to do it tonight." My voice strained as I tried to rally strength out of her.

"What?"

"Kill you!"

"Good." She couldn't find the energy to utter more than a word to me, as if there was a limit to how many she had left. Maybe there was.

"Mouse, come on! You can't—"

She dropped her head again. She was broken.

"God damn it!" I rubbed my hand through my hair as I paced on my chain.

I don't know what to do.

Her arm had bent backwards in an awkward position, and I couldn't help but wonder if it was out of its socket, her body too tired to acknowledge the pain. She swayed beneath her arm. I stared at her chest, watching for the steady rise and fall beneath the gown. The shadows blocked my view. Maybe she was already gone. And maybe it would be better if she was.

"Mouse?" I asked, trying to get her to show some sign of life.

She groaned in response.

I leaned toward her, stretching the skin of my wrist beneath the manacle. "I'm sorry. I'd do anything to save you. If I had been free, this wouldn't have happened. I wouldn't let it happen. I would have done whatever I had to do." My voice shook. "I'm not the person I was before you got here. You showed me what love feels like, and I'll never feel that again. I'm sorry I told you I regretted it. I don't regret it. I would take a bullet to my forehead if it meant I could be with you like that again. To be able to hold you and kiss you. To listen to your sassy, smart-mouthed remarks."

I took a deep breath after pouring my heart out in a rambling mess, unsure if she heard any of it. If she had, she didn't respond.

I scooted back against the wall and looked at the boxes to

my left. I'd glanced at them before. They held old Christmas ornaments on hooks too rusted to be of any use. Still, I had to try something. I dug through the box with my free hand. An ornament shattered beneath my fingers and sliced through my skin.

"Fuck!" I yanked my hand to my mouth, nearly knocking the box over. I leaned back against the wall and looked at the cut. Blood swelled and dripped toward my elbow.

From the corner of my eye, I saw a glint of metal behind the boxes. I grabbed it and pulled it toward me, revealing an old hacksaw. The metal was weak and rusted, but it was better than a Christmas ornament.

I tucked my chain under my foot to keep the links taut, and sawed at the section near the plate in the wall. I stopped frequently to listen for footsteps or the door. The metal teased me with separation, but the blade struggled with its age. With my tongue between my teeth, I worked at it until my arm was sore.

"Come the fuck on!"

The locks on the basement door rattled, and I made a few more hurried passes over the chain before shoving the saw back behind the box. The links hung together by a sliver of metal. With a few more passes, it would have broken apart.

Fuck. I sighed and dropped my head back.

Marcy appeared in the doorway. She smiled, walked to the table, and lit an extra candle. She strolled to Mackenzie and wrapped her fingers through her hair. With a snatch of her wrist, she pulled back Mackenzie's head. Her eyes locked on to the rise and fall of her chest.

"Guess she didn't go on her own, huh?" Marcy said. "Are you as excited as I am, Benjamin? Soon, it will just be us again." She shook her head. "I'm sorry I ever brought her here."

Marcy continued examining Mackenzie's tired body. I

dared to glance at the boxes. There was no way to quietly saw through the remaining strip of metal. I'd have to think of something else.

"Yeah, I'm really excited," I said as I sat back and picked up the chain. My fingers wrestled with the frayed and twisted metal. Sweat formed on my forehead and dripped down my temples. "Tell me what she looks like, Marcy. Describe her to me in detail."

"Oh, she looks absolutely pitiful," Marcy said with a sadistic smile on her face. "She's hardly breathing. Another few hours and she'll be dead for sure."

"Marcy?" I called, drawing her attention to me. "Will you kiss her for me? I want to see that before she's gone."

Marcy turned toward Mackenzie and stroked her cheek. She leaned in and placed her lips against Mackenzie's mouth.

I kept checking over my shoulder as I twisted the links with as much strength as I could muster. The jagged metal tore at my fingertips, but I kept twisting and wiggling. The chain rattled along the ground with every twist of my wrist.

I raised my voice to cover the sound. "I want you to touch her." I apologized to Mackenzie a hundred times over in my head.

Marcy dropped her hand to Mackenzie's chest, caressing her nipples through the fabric of the gown. Marcy bit her lip as an excited moan built in her chest.

"Yeah, just like that." I projected my voice as loud as I could without raising suspicion. "Kiss her again," I said, hiding the panic in my voice.

Marcy obliged and spread Mackenzie's lips with her tongue.

"God, that's so incredible, Marcy."

The chain split in two and sped toward the ground. I grabbed it before it could clatter against the concrete. I took a sharp breath and wiped the blood from my damaged fingers against my pants.

Marcy wiped her mouth with the back of her hand. "That's enough fun," she whispered as she took a step back. Her fingers wrapped around the butt of the pistol. She lifted it, aiming the barrel toward Mackenzie's head. "Go ahead, Benjamin. Say goodbye."

"Are you sure we have to do this?" I leaned forward and got to my knees.

Marcy nodded as she cocked the pistol. "Yes, we have to. It's the only way."

I climbed to my feet, careful to keep the chain still and silent. I crept toward her.

Do it. You have to do it.

I wound the chain's tail around my hand and took a deep breath. My legs pushed me forward in a rush. Before she knew what was happening, I had the cold metal around her throat. The gun went off. She dropped the pistol and reached for her neck, gripping at the rusted links pressed against her windpipe. Her nails dug into the skin around the chain. She writhed violently against me, and I struggled to maintain my grip. Her fingers shot toward my face. I leaned back to avoid her touch, but her nails caught my cheek, taking a chunk of flesh with them. Veins protruded around her forehead. Blood vessels strained and popped within her wide eyes, staining the whites. The sight of her silent screams made my stomach heave as her grasp grew weaker. She struggled for a final breath, but I wouldn't allow an ounce of oxygen to enter her lungs. My hands shook, but I refused to let go. I held her until she went limp against me.

I am not a killer. But I killed her.

"Goodbye," I whispered, finally responding to the request she meant for Mackenzie.

I released the chain from my hand and Marcy fell to the

floor with a thud. I stared at her for a moment, something like guilt mixing with happiness brewing inside me.

Mackenzie coughed. I remembered why I was there. Who I was fighting for. Who I killed for.

I rushed to her side. "Mouse!"

I lifted her head and examined her body to see if she'd been shot. Her eyes rolled in their sockets, unable to focus on my face.

Marcy gasped and coughed on the floor. My eyes widened and locked on the gun as I turned around. It lay inches from Marcy's fingers. She reached for it, her mouth open as if trying to speak.

I snatched the gun away before she could get her fingers around it.

"Why?" Marcy said in a hoarse whisper.

I cocked the hammer and aimed the barrel at Marcy's head.

"No!" she choked out as she looked up at me.

Her eyes begged for mercy. It was the same look she loved to see from others. I wanted to look away, but I had to see it. I had to watch her die. I pulled the trigger. The sound crashed against the basement walls, leaving my ears ringing. The bullet seared through Marcy's skull. Her blood and brains flew in gooey chunks from the back of her head and spread around her. I lowered the pistol and dropped it to the ground.

Marcy was flat on her belly, the crimson liquid pouring from her head. I took a deep breath and dipped my hand into her pocket. Nothing. I reached beneath her and wiggled my fingers into the other pocket, avoiding the blood as it snaked toward my sneakers.

I caught a glimpse of the side of her face, mangled and unrecognizable. For a moment, I felt like part of me took a last breath when she did. I hoped it had. That part of me deserved to die as much as Marcy.

My fingers wrapped around the keyring. It jangled as I pulled it from Marcy's pocket. I rushed to free Mackenzie, trying several of the rounded brass keys before I found the right one. Once I unclasped the lock, I grabbed the end of the chain and carefully lowered her limp body to the ground. I fell beside her and wrapped her up in my arms. I lifted her face with one hand and put my ear to her mouth, hoping to feel or hear her breath.

"Took you long enough," she mumbled.

I chuckled and held her close to my chest. "Smart ass mouth," I said as I rocked her. I picked her up, cradling her and trying to shield her view as we passed Marcy's lifeless body.

"I want to see her," she whispered through cracked lips. She batted at my hands and tried to lean over to look at the ground.

As much as I didn't want her to see Marcy's dead body, Mackenzie had a reason to look. Marcy was her nightmare, and she needed to make sure the boogeyman beneath her bed was really gone. Though I was no archangel rescuing her from evil. I was just the lesser of the two evils.

Mackenzie used all her strength to open her eyes and take in the scene before her. A smile crept across her face. She released a contented sigh and relaxed into my arms. I took the steps cautiously, as if she were a fragile piece of glass. I had never held anything so delicate and precious in my arms. I placed her on the couch and took a step back.

What now?

Getting rid of Marcy was only a first step. We were still prisoners within the house.

Chapter Twenty-Three

MACKENZIE

I struggled to open my heavy eyelids. They felt as if they weighed no less than one hundred pounds. I looked down and saw no chain on my arm. My head swam as I fought to sit up, unsure how I got to the couch, where Marcy was, or if I was even still alive.

What the hell happened?

I blinked away the mental fog and looked toward the armchair where Benjamin slept. Unchained. His soft and sporadic snores broke the quiet. Since he was beside me, I knew I was still alive. We wouldn't have ended up in the same afterlife.

"Benjamin," I whispered.

He startled awake, rubbing his eyes as he sat up. He walked to the couch and sat beside me, reaching out and tracing his fingers along my shoulder.

I tensed at his affection. "What happened?"

His gaze dropped, focusing on the blood which painted his shoe. "I killed Marcy."

"What?" My mouth fell open. It shouldn't have surprised me. The only way we'd be upstairs—unchained and alive—would be if she were dead. *He chose me over her. Oh god.*

"I had to. She was going to kill you." Benjamin shook his head. "What do you remember?"

I shrugged. "I don't know. I remember her chaining me to the rafter. I don't remember much else."

"So, you don't remember me saying anything?" he asked casually.

I smiled at him. "Oh, you mean when you professed your love for me?"

"Jesus Christ." Benjamin rubbed his hand through his hair.

"I remember most of it. I remember you having her kiss me. Thanks for that." I pursed my lips with disgust.

"I didn't know what else to have her do to distract her while I broke the chain. I had to keep her from getting to her gun." He took a soft breath. "Let me make us something to eat." Benjamin touched my shoulder once more before standing up and going into the kitchen.

I sat in disbelief as I heard the sizzling of eggs in a pan. My wrist was raw and bruised—probably sprained—and my shoulder wasn't much better. I opened and closed my mouth, moving thick, gummy saliva over my tongue. I needed water. As if he'd read my mind, Benjamin appeared with a tall glass in his hand.

He held it toward me. "You'll start to feel a little better once you drink some water. You're dehydrated." He returned to the kitchen.

I guzzled the metallic-tinged liquid. The cold cannonball of water slammed into my hollow gut, and I fought off the urge to vomit.

Benjamin came back with two pan-fried eggs and a fork, and handed them to me. My shoulder throbbed as I lifted the plate from his hands. My body remembered everything. It was easy enough to ignore the pain—hardly a blip compared to the discomfort I endured thus far.

"There were only two eggs left," he said.

"Take one." I offered half to Benjamin.

He pushed the plate back toward me. "No, you need it more than me."

I hesitated for a moment before shoveling food into my mouth. "Why haven't we gotten out of here?" I asked through a mouthful of egg.

"There's a problem. The keys for the door aren't on Marcy's key ring. They're somewhere in the house, but she always hid them from me. I had to wait in the bathroom each time she came home so I wouldn't see where she kept them."

"Are you fucking kidding me?" I put the plate on the aged coffee table and dropped my pounding head into my hands. The hope of escape dissolved like snow dropped in water.

"There's not a lot of food here either. If we can't find the key soon, we're going to starve."

I stared straight ahead in disbelief. I shook my head as my odor wafted toward my nose. "Can I take a shower?"

I was still pissed off about everything—his pitch-black past, hanging like a damn puppet from the rafters, and remaining stuck in the house—but all I wanted was to feel clean. I at least had control over that much.

I tried to get to my feet, but my legs gave out and sent me to the floor. Benjamin hurried to my side, scooped me up, and carried me to the bathroom. Once he situated me on the toilet, he lifted the gown over my head and held me steady as he turned on the water. The old pipes rattled before the stream trickled from the showerhead. The sound and the steam revitalized my tired muscles. I stood on unsteady legs and climbed into the tub with his help. The water reddened my skin as I leaned against the wall.

The door closed, and Benjamin's shadow moved behind the moldy shower curtain. He stripped off his clothes and pushed the curtain aside, staring at my body before stepping in. The heat made him recoil for a moment before he eased himself under the water. A groan left his lips.

I didn't want to shower with him. I hardly wanted to be around him at all. But I was too tired to fight him.

Benjamin grabbed the soap and washed his body before handing it to me. I cleaned myself, but instead of rushing like he had, I savored the moment and washed the filth from my skin with slow, deliberate movements. The memories washed away at my feet.

I put the soap down and turned toward Benjamin. His arms wrapped around me and pulled me close. I stood with my arms at my side, still confused after the things I heard in the basement. He was a rapist. He wasn't a good guy. But he also killed for me. He murdered the only person he'd cared about for years.

"Thank you for saving me," I whispered as I leaned into his chest. My body felt too tired to hold myself up any longer. I hadn't forgiven him—I didn't know if I could—but I needed the familiarity of his touch.

"You saved me too, mouse, but we still aren't free."

"I know, but that had to have been hard for you. To kill Marcy," I said as I looked up at him.

He closed his eyes. The water ran down his forehead and dripped from his lashes. "I know it had to be done, but pieces of me died with her."

"Hopefully the rapist pieces." My lips turned up in a smirk.

I imagined Marcy holding shreds of him in her shaking hands as she walked through Hell's gate to greet her master. All the parts of him that wouldn't let him be vulnerable. All the false feelings he had for Marcy. I hoped she carried the weight of his torture and manipulation on her back, weighing her down for eternity.

"Ah, there's the comedian, back for an encore." He grinned at me. "Guess we'll find out, won't we?"

I tensed as Benjamin reached behind me and turned off the water. The pipes rattled again as the last drops fell from the showerhead. His hand grazed my hip as he dropped his arm to his side. My naked body was against him, and I expected him to try to fuck me. Instead, he took a step back and wrung out his hair.

I stepped out first and grabbed a towel. A set of clean clothes waited on the bathroom counter—real clothes, not just some skimpy gown. I picked up the shirt and put it over my head before grabbing the pants and slipping them on. I had to roll the waistband a bit to keep them up. I looked at myself in the mirror. My hands grazed the scabbed-over cuts on my face. My shaking fingers sifted through strands of short, choppy hair.

"Oh god," I whispered.

Benjamin stepped out of the shower and lifted the clothes he brought in for himself. He grabbed a beanie hat sandwiched between the shirt and the pants, and placed it on my head.

"Don't worry about it." He tugged the hat down, looking into my eyes as he released the fabric. "I would still fuck the almighty hell out of you."

The heat of impending tears scalded my eyes. I felt hideous.

"You look the same as the day I met you." He placed a heavy hand on top of my bony shoulder. "Relax."

I looked at my scarred hands and reached toward my back to touch the scars from my beating. *Nothing about me is the same.*

He caught me in an embrace and held me up as my shoulders dropped. The weak mouse being coddled by the wolf. What a juxtaposition. Droplets of water dripped down his chest. The bullet wound in his shoulder hadn't fully healed yet, and pink branches of skin twisted around the edges of the indention—a reminder of the sacrifice he'd been willing to make.

His fingers wrapped around my chin and lifted my face. "All I want to do is take you into the living room and show you how attractive you are to me, but I'm trying so fucking hard to stop myself. I can still taste you on my tongue."

My lip trembled at the passion dripping from his words. "I don't want that," I whispered. I didn't. I still wasn't certain about my feelings, and that wasn't how I wanted to explore them.

Benjamin wrapped his hand around the back of my neck and pulled me into him. "I know. Whenever you feel bad about your body, just remember that I would devour you in half a heartbeat. If you let me, I would show you just how much I ache for you. You fuck with my mind, mouse."

His gravelly voice sent a shiver rolling through my body. It was hard for him to control his impulses. He was like a dog with no bite inhibition. He wouldn't just nip me; he'd rip me apart.

"I need to lie down." I sighed and pushed the confused feelings away.

Benjamin picked me up and carried me to the couch. He placed me down and covered me with a scratchy blanket. He fetched another glass of water. I guzzled it down, my heavy eyelids closed, and I welcomed sleep.

I WOKE UP AND STRETCHED. Benjamin was awake in the chair beside me. His rigid posture and shaking leg told me something was bothering him.

"Morning," I said with a yawn.

He didn't respond. The heel of his sneaker tapped on the hardwood. He looked as though the weight of everything hit him while I was asleep.

I sat up and scooted back against the couch, drawing my knees up. I wrapped my arms around my legs and ignored the pain still ripping through my shoulder. A wave of guilt washed through me, as if I was to blame for it all. I didn't ask him to kill Marcy for me. I had resigned myself to my fate.

"We need to find the key," he said. He stood and started to walk away, but I grabbed the back of his shirt. He spun on his heels and ripped the fabric from my hands before heading into the kitchen.

I followed him. "Benjamin, stop!" I stumbled in front of him as he started looking through drawers.

"What, Mackenzie?" he snapped.

He never called me by my name. His anger made me feel confused and nervous. Either he was actually upset with me, or he knew the situation was more dire than I thought.

"Why are you being like this to me?"

His eyes narrowed. "Step aside."

I dug my heels into the shitty laminate floors and braced my arm against the counter. "No."

"I'm not getting into this with you right now."

"I thought you—"

He grabbed my shoulders and forced me backward, pinning me against the wall. The corded phone rattled beside my head, and the frayed wires popping from the base scratched at my shoulder.

"I thought I was different. That I could be different for you." He drew a deep breath. "But I still have dark thoughts.

I still have desires I shouldn't. Like right now, I want you so fucking bad." His pelvis pressed against me, his hardness apparent as it rubbed through his jeans against my stomach. "I watched you sleep. I had such *sick* fantasies."

I swallowed hard. "But you didn't do anything to me. You *are* different. *You* held yourself back from me. Not Marcy. You."

He leaned in and pushed a rough and passionate kiss against my lips. He drew away from me and searched my eyes. Our foreheads touched as he breathed me in.

I wasn't afraid of him. I stood taller and faced his aggression head on. I knew in my heart he wouldn't hurt me. He wouldn't take me against my will, no matter how much his body or mind beckoned him. There would be a learning curve —a reconditioning period where he would be more confused about what he wanted. I was trapped in the house with him and his temptations, but I still felt safe in his arms because I knew he would rise above his demons.

He released me and backed away. He rubbed a hand through his hair and focused on his breathing. I controlled the throb between my legs by rifling through drawers in search of the key.

We opened cabinets and checked under drawers. I picked up a cookie jar with white doves flying across it. I checked under it and found a silver key taped to the bottom. I pulled it off and walked over to the door, but I couldn't quite reach the lock myself. Benjamin sighed and took the key from me. When he put the key in the lock, it wouldn't turn.

"No dice," he said as he dropped the key into my palm. "I knew it wouldn't be that easy."

"What do you think it belongs to?"

"Not a clue. Marcy kept everything secret from me."

We moved to the living room next, lifting cushions and

checking on and below the windowsills. Benjamin tipped the TV and checked underneath but found only dust.

"It's not here," he said. "Let's check upstairs."

I dropped onto the couch, already exhausted. "Upstairs? Shouldn't we check the bedroom down here first?"

He shook his head. "I checked it last night while you were sleeping. Thought about crashing on the mattress because that chair is uncomfortable as fuck, but I didn't want you to wake up alone."

"I don't know how you can be in that room so easily. How do you go in there while knowing all the pain you caused people?"

"Mouse." Benjamin sat down beside me, but I scooted away. "Please don't."

"I'm thankful for what you've done for me, but it doesn't negate what you've done to others."

"I was a bad person. You knew this, and you still fell for me. There's no excuse for what I've done." He sighed. "All I can do is find that damn key and get us out of here. Even if it means going into that bedroom and reminding myself of how bad I was." He reached out to touch my arm, and I recoiled. My reaction twisted his expression, as if I stabbed a knife into his gut and swirled it around. "I'm not asking you to forgive me or be with me. Don't worry."

He stared at me as we processed our feelings. The pendulum shifted as we stifled emotions we didn't need to have. I wanted him to touch me, but I needed him to stop putting his hands on me. When I wanted to hate him, I found myself needing to love him. He'd done unmentionable things, but I wanted to be the one to wiggle into his heart and stroke the beast inside him.

"Come on. Let's check upstairs," he said as he stood up.

"What's up there?" I asked.

"The bedroom Marcy and I shared."

I nodded and followed him to the old mahogany staircase.

Each riser let out a groan on our way to the upstairs bedroom. Benjamin opened the door, and a whoosh of stagnant, cold air rushed toward us. I looked around at the clutter with wide eyes. Clothing, tables, and knickknacks stretched toward the ceiling.

"We aren't going to find that key if it's in this mess," I said as I kicked over dolls and trash.

Benjamin turned toward me with sullen eyes. "That's what I'm afraid of."

While Benjamin tossed items around, I lay back on the bed and watched the ceiling fan spin sluggishly above me. Intrusive images of Benjamin fucking Marcy clouded my mind, and I fought to push them away. If I never heard her theatrical moans again, it would be too soon. And I wouldn't hear them again because she was dead. In the basement.

I smiled.

Benjamin lifted a small lock box from a pile of debris in the closet. Clothes tumbled to his feet as he stepped toward me. He brought it over to the bed and set it down. "Do you still have that key?" he asked.

I fished around in my pockets and handed him the small silver key. He placed it in the lock and turned it. The lock clicked. The lid creaked as it opened, and I craned my head to look inside. Folded yellow paper filled the space to the brim. I reached in, picked one up, and began to read it.

Dear Diary,

Today is another day in the bedroom. He keeps me chained to the headboard for his convenience. He has sex with me every single day now. I hate it. I hate him. God doesn't seem willing to answer my prayers, so I don't bother anymore. Why me? I was just walking home. I didn't bother no one. Why did I get in the car? I will always wonder about that. I'm going to die here, and I hope whoever reads this letter will find my body and let my family know.

Signed,

Marcy

I put a hand over my mouth. "Benjamin, read this!" I handed it to him and watched as his eyes scanned the paper.

"Oh my god." He sank onto the bed and flipped the paper over. "It's dated June 5, 1990."

I picked up another folded square. "This one was dated August 13, 1991," I said as I opened it and flipped it over. I read it out loud.

Dear Diary,

My captor performed an abortion on me at home today. I was a couple months late. The procedure didn't go well, and I keep bleeding. He said he hopes that there's enough scar tissue to keep me from getting pregnant again. It was the worst pain. I thought this would give me a break from sex, but it's still happening. I prayed to God to take me home, but He isn't listening. I still woke up in this bed, chained and bleeding. He said if I get pregnant again, he will kill me. If He is real, please don't make me pregnant again.

Signed,

Marcy

"Oh god, Benjamin. Do you know what this means?" I looked at him with wide eyes. "Marcy was a victim too."

"How? Why? These can't be real. She was able to come and go freely when she took my sister and me. Why wouldn't she get out when she had the chance?"

"Remember when we talked about being Stockholmed? She must have been really fucking Stockholmed." I sighed.

"Why would she kidnap people for him? Why would she

make me do those things to them, even with Benjamin gone? It doesn't make sense."

"Sometimes victims become the perpetrators. It's a vicious cycle. Don't forget, you were on that path too."

"No . . . I," he stammered. "I'm not like *this*."

I tightened my lips. "You were."

A single tear rolled down his face. It dripped onto the letter in his hands, smearing the ink. "I killed her, and she just wanted to be loved," Benjamin whispered.

"Benjamin, don't do that. No. She chose her path, and you chose yours. She wanted to continue to hurt people, and she would have kept going until she was stopped." I touched his hand for a moment before withdrawing from him.

"I know, but—"

"But nothing. She was going to kill me. You're feeling sympathy for Marcy the victim, and that's okay, but that's not who's lying in the basement right now."

Benjamin dipped his hand in the box and ran his fingers through dozens of letters. Years of abuse at his fingertips.

"There's no key in there, mouse. Close it up."

He pushed the box toward me, and I closed it. He stood, picked it up, and tried to stuff it back into the closet. An avalanche of useless shit fell around him. A cardboard box landed at his feet, spreading its contents across the carpet. Benjamin sat on the ground and sifted through the items. He picked up some clothing, clutching a shirt to his chest.

"What is it?" I asked.

"My sister's shirt." He lifted it up to his face and sniffed. "It still smells a little like her." He looked through the other women's clothing in the box, his face full of recognition. "How did we sleep in here every night with all these haunting memories tucked away? How did the spirits ever let us rest?"

The size of Shit Mountain helped me see how difficult it

would be to find the key. It felt impossible. My thoughts swirled as I wondered why he wasn't panicking more. Did he know where the key was? Did he have it all along? He said he searched the bedroom downstairs. Was he keeping it from me to hold me in place?

"Benjamin?" I paused, afraid to ask the question. "You aren't hiding the key to keep me here, are you?"

He dropped the shirt. It tumbled to the floor and landed between his feet as he stood. He leaned forward, placing his hands on either side of my face as a look of hurt blanketed his eyes.

"No. Forcing someone to be with you doesn't make them love you. You taught me that. I want to find the key as much as you do."

My eyes welled with tears and spilled over my cheeks and onto his hands. "I want to believe you. I do. But you were conditioned to hurt and control women."

"Mouse," he whispered, "I don't know how else to prove it to you but to find that key and let you walk out that door."

My eyes rounded with a torn sadness. I wanted to leave. I wanted to leave that all behind. Forget about the pain and heartbreak. But I didn't want to leave Benjamin. As twisted as it was, I couldn't imagine a life without him once he became the center of mine. He loved me to the core of his being. I could let go of everything he'd ever done and tear apart the history that blurred the line between Benjamin and Dylan. I could love the one who burned all he ever knew for me.

His finger grazed the sticky wet skin of my cheeks. "I won't stand in your way. I promise you. She hid the key so I wouldn't find it. The basement locks were for you, but those locks on the front and back doors were for me."

Chapter Twenty-Four

BENJAMIN

I glanced sideways at Mackenzie every so often. Her legs were crossed under her as she fisted a bag of chips. One of the last bags of anything substantial in the damn house. I was panicking a bit, but I couldn't show her that. She held the bag out to me, but I shook my head.

"Really?" She jiggled the bag. "There's not a lot of food left."

I sighed and reached in, grabbing a few of the salty, stale chips and eating them. I wiped oily fingerprints onto the remote as I changed the channel.

I wanted to protect her with everything in me, but I couldn't find the one thing we needed. Part of me wondered if I looked hard enough. I wanted her to stay with me, and if she couldn't leave, she would stay mine. I could use her whenever the urge struck. But I refused to repeat the cycle and become someone like Marcy. I cared about my mouse too much to do that. If she didn't choose to stay with me, I'd live with the memories of her. They would keep me warm at night and drive me insane for the rest of my days.

"We need to find that key, or we're going to die a slow death in here," I said.

She shrugged. "Well, at least we aren't dying while locked in the basement. That's a plus."

I rolled my eyes. "I'm finding your smart mouth less than appealing right now." I wiped my fingers off on my jeans as she tipped the bag into her mouth to get the last of the crumbs.

"Well, it's true. I'd rather be up here with you. Being that close to death down there, you learn what's worth getting upset over. Am I worried? Yeah. But I also never thought I'd leave this place alive." She shrugged. "The only thing changing would be the way I died, and even if we starve, it's better than being chained half-naked on stained concrete and dying at the hands of Marcy."

"I guess."

I dropped my head against my fist and focused on the television. Mackenzie leaned back and stretched, her pert nipples rubbing against the fabric of her shirt. The more stressed I got, the more I thought about where to dump that stress. And I wanted it to be inside her. She looked up at me with bright blue eyes renewed with life, and it made me hard as fuck. I still imagined those eyes looking up at me as she sucked my cock. *Oh god.*

Her hand reached over and rested on my lap.

"Be careful with that, mouse."

"Why?" she asked with innocence on her face, as if she didn't know I'd be all over her and have my mouth on every inch of her if she didn't stop.

"Keep rubbing that, and I'll remind you what it felt like when I fucked you." I bit into my lower lip, trying to control my urges. The animal inside me paced on its chain. "Or better yet, I'll finally take that smart mouth of yours."

She looked at me with a trembling lip. Her cheeks flushed, and a battle raged within her. If we were going to die, we could at least go out in a blaze of orgasms. But I wasn't going to push the matter, no matter how much my mouth watered for it.

I grabbed her arm and tugged her to the ground between my legs. I wasn't going to push the matter, but I sure as shit might suggest it. I rubbed my finger along her lower lip, twitching at the thought of finally having her on willing knees.

The animal inside me tugged at the chain, gnashing his mighty jaws. I wanted to grab what was left of her hair and force myself past her soft, full lips. I kept my hands at my sides. If she didn't want to give it, I wouldn't take it.

I won't. The balls are in your court, mouse.

She hesitated for a few moments before her hand worked my pants open. She looked up at me, and if I hadn't felt the warm breath of her along my cock as she pulled me from my boxers, I would have thought I was dreaming. I grabbed the back of her head to keep her from disappearing before I could feel her mouth on me.

She took me into her mouth, and it was like Heaven and Hell merged and the demons danced with the angels. It was like everything and nothing I dreamed of. She was better than my sick mind could conjure.

Fuck her throat.

I shook my head. *Don't do anything to make her pull away.*

Even if she does, if you're fucking her mouth, she can't get far.

I want her to want me.

I argued with my own desperate desire. I kept my hand against the back of her head, but I didn't force anything. She ran her tongue along the length of me, swirling it around the head of my cock. I throbbed as she took me as deep into her mouth as she could. I felt the back of her throat. She sucked me, drawing all the pleasure up from my balls. I didn't want to come in her mouth, though. No. I wanted to fill her pussy. Remind her what was mine, even once she walked out of there.

I pulled her onto my lap. "Can I kiss you?"

She looked taken aback by my question.

"Is that a no?" I leaned away from her.

"No . . . yes . . . I mean, yes, you can." She nodded, the shocked look still plastered on her face.

I wrapped my hand around her neck and kissed her. A heated kiss that even made the beast howl. I couldn't get her shirt off fast enough before I let my mouth race over her skin. She felt so fragile and small in my hands, but I still grasped and squeezed every arch and curve of her body. I wanted her more than I wanted freedom.

I pushed her off me, leaning over her as her stomach pressed against the couch. My fingers walked along the waistband of her pants, and I pulled them down as I pulled her ass toward me. I lifted her up to me, rubbing an unwavering hand down her chest. My cock throbbed against her hot skin.

"Are you okay with this?" I whispered with a growl in her ear.

Her body screamed that it was—from the arching of her back to the sheen of excitement between her legs—but I wanted to hear her say it. I needed to know she wanted me. She nodded.

"Tell me," I commanded as I rubbed myself against her.

Her breath hitched. "I want you to fuck me."

I gave her exactly what she wanted. I sank inside her. She stretched around me, welcoming me into the depths of her. She spasmed as I slammed my hips against her ass. She was so warm and inviting. A wet embrace that pulled me deeper.

She was everything. Her pussy was so good, I considered keeping her all over again.

Her melodic moans danced in my ears. They blocked out every other sick sound inside my mind. They silenced the cries and smothered my past.

I reached a hand around her throat while the other drifted between her legs to rub her clit. I wanted to make her come. I wanted to feel her tighten around me so I could come with her. She was so sensitive to my touch, dropping her face into the arm of the couch to fight the overpowering sensations.

I lifted her by her throat. "Don't fight it, mouse." My voice was primal and animalistic, and it made her tremble.

I pulled her into me as I rubbed her. Her body shook in my grasp, fighting her orgasm.

"Come," I growled in her ear.

I slammed into her once more, sending her over the edge as she screamed out. She shuddered against me, every muscle inside her tightening around me and drawing out every drop of come. I rubbed her until she twitched and pleaded for me to stop. I loved hearing her beg.

I kept myself inside her, trying to savor the feeling of her around me in case this would be the last time. Her whimpers reached into my pelvis, climbed my spine like a ladder, and nestled into my heart. I wasn't positive she reciprocated the feelings I had for her, but when her body responded to mine, I could pretend.

I collapsed beside her on the couch, my heavily scarred arms wrapped around her waist.

"Wow," she whispered. "Where did you learn to fuck like that?" She paused. "Never mind, don't answer that. There's not a single answer I'd want to hear."

If she thought I learned what I knew from any of the women I'd had beneath me—including Marcy—she'd only be half right. Marcy taught me how to fuck, but my heart was never truly in it. Once I felt the way my heart beat around Mackenzie, I realized everything I'd ever known had been fabricated. An illusion. My thrusts were stronger and deeper as I mimicked the pulse in my ears. My kiss was passionate, something that was once so taboo and foreign. It was like learning a new language. The words rolled over my tongue and spilled into her mouth.

"You're the one who taught me how to fuck like that. No one else."

She turned over and looked at me. "You never fucked Marcy like that?"

"Not once. Sex with her was like a job. There wasn't anything primal like there is with you. There was never so much heat between us that I thought we'd start a fire." I growled against the crook of her neck. "I don't know if this is love, but it's something in the same realm, on the same planet, and that's the closest I'll ever get. Once we leave this place, I know you'll move on from me, and I understand. If I were you, I wouldn't want to be with a constant reminder of this place, either."

"Don't count yourself out quite yet." She smiled as she brushed my hair back with her fingers.

We sat entwined at the hips for so long, I lost track of time. I would lay forever with the remnants of her on my dick if I could have.

"Question." She looked up at me. "What's with all the snow globes in the bedroom?"

I cocked my head at her. "Where the hell did that come from?"

"I've been wanting to know. I thought I would die while never knowing why a psychopath like Marcy has three hundred fucking snow globes."

"Okay, you may enjoy the answer, then." I smirked. "Marcy's main goal in life was to collect every bird snow globe on the market. No joke. Every one of them."

"Why?" she asked with a raised eyebrow.

"She just really fucking liked birds." I laughed and rubbed a hand through my hair.

Oh god. Guilt ripped through my mind as I thought about Marcy, dead in the basement. My stomach lurched at the thought of having to take care of her like we had with the women beneath the tree. If we could ever find the damn key.

"I have to pee," Mackenzie said as she stood on shaky legs.

She hopped on one foot, trying to fight the sudden urge. She stumbled back and bumped into the table holding the TV. Trying too hard to right herself, she ended up knocking a picture frame off the stand. It fell to the ground and shattered. I stood and zipped my pants.

I looked down at the picture—one of Marcy and me, our faces pressed together. Her smile was full and proud, and mine was so clearly forced. I hadn't noticed it before. A crack ran through the middle of the glass, spreading between us.

Mackenzie steadied herself against the wall and tossed me a rushed apology as she ran to the bathroom.

I lifted the frame by the corners. The soft back piece fell away and landed on my foot. I picked it up and turned the frame over to place it back together. Taped to the back of the picture was a shining silver key. My eyes widened as I carefully peeled it off, holding it in my open hand.

If I had any interest in hiding the key from Mackenzie, I needed to do it before she returned. The conditioned side of me threatened to rear its head, not quite ready for this to end. All I had to do was slip the key into my pocket and close the frame. I wouldn't have to worry about saying goodbye to her. Not yet, at least. The parts of me she'd reconditioned radiated with guilt at the thought.

"Why do you look like that?" Mackenzie asked as she appeared in the doorway.

I couldn't lie to her. If she wanted to be with me, it had to be her choice.

"I think I found the key." I picked it up and held it so she could see. Metallic freedom between my fingertips. I made a promise to her, and I didn't intend to break it, no matter how my thoughts tempted me.

Her mouth dropped open. "Is it really?"

I walked toward the front door. My hand shook as I put the key into the lock. The keyhole accepted it willingly. I turned the key, and the lock clicked.

I stopped. Mackenzie sucked in a breath behind me as I turned around and put my back against the cool door. I reached out for her, but she took a hesitant step back. She was scared I might keep her. That I wouldn't let her go now that the opportunity had so generously presented itself.

"Mouse." I stepped into her, forcing her back against the wall.

Her eyes were rounded with a hint of fear. It hardened me somehow, in a way that sucked me out of that room and dropped me back into the bedroom.

That's not me anymore.

I tried to rationalize, but who was I kidding? It *was* me. There wasn't a day that went by where I hadn't wanted her, whether she wanted me back or not. If she stayed with me, every day would be a fight to force back the monster inside me and make him walk instead of run for her.

My hand snaked around the back of her neck and fisted her mangled hair. "You're mine. Even if you walk out of here and never look back, you're mine. I'll think about fucking you. I'll crave your mouth." I rubbed my thumb along her lips. "For the rest of my life."

Her lip trembled. "What could we possibly be?"

Everything. We could be everything. I'd be the hurricane while she was the grass weathering my storm. I'd be the wildfire while she doused me until I was unable to burn her. She would be the drug that tamed the beast, leaving him curled up on the floor between us. He would never go away, his growl a constant reminder of his presence, but he wouldn't threaten to devour her whole anymore. She'd feed him enough of herself to satisfy him and lull him to sleep.

"We could be this." I leaned into her and kissed her until her body relaxed and she melted into my chest. I spread her lips until she stopped fearing me. I tasted her until she knew I'd burn that house down for her. I never wanted to let her go.

I had half a mind to scoop her up and keep her from leaving. Ensure she was mine and that no one would ever feel her pussy besides me. She pulled away from me, her cheeks flushing. I expected her to reject me. I prepared myself to control the urge to chain her ass up again and give her no choice but to love me.

"I'm sorry for everything I've ever done to you, and things I didn't do for you, but I can't do this without you." I hated to show her how much I needed her, but I fucking *needed* her. She was the breath in my lungs, the blood surging through my veins. She was the beat in my heart. I'd keep my promise to her that she could leave. As lifeless as it'd make me, the decision lay with her. "What do you want, mouse?"

The pink hue from her cheeks crawled down her neck and mottled her chest. "You," she whispered. Her gaze dropped as if she felt guilty for choosing me. As she should have.

"Mackenzie, I'm not going to hurt you. I'm not going to force you to stay here or be with me. This is your chance to say what you really want. I won't hold it against you." *I'd hold it all against myself.*

She flashed her blue eyes at me, the fear washed away

from them. I touched her cheek, feeling her pulse beneath my hand.

"You are what I want, Benjamin."

Benjamin. The word tainted my tongue. I didn't want to hear her say the name, let alone utter it in desire or scream it out in pleasure as I buried myself between her legs. Despite the roar of protest in my head, I pulled her into me and kissed her.

"Call me Dylan," I said through a tensed jaw. "Benjamin is dead."

Epilogue

Ten months later

Benjamin

How had so much time passed without me noticing a day of it? Maybe because I didn't fear captivity. I knew how to live within the confines I'd been given. An alarm buzzed overhead as a big metal door unlocked and opened. The officer led me to the processing area without a glance in my direction.

Would she even recognize me? My hair was much shorter. My face was almost clean shaved. I couldn't let go of everything I used to be. Not yet. My muscles tugged at the sleeves of the shirt I came in with. I filled out more than just the arms. I gained weight where I needed to. Ten months in prison? It was nothing. It was much less than I deserved.

I owned up to what I could. Mackenzie's testimony was damning—not to me, but to Marcy. She was the puppeteer, and I had been the puppet. It made me sound weak.

I was weak.

When I lay alone in my cell, listening to the screams of other inmates, I thought about Marcy. She still had such a hold on me. Even with her body long gone, she haunted the recesses of my mind. Even her ghost refused to let me go.

Stockholmed. That's what the therapist called me. I didn't see it like that at first, but I see it now. Once I left the property of the state, I would belong to no one but myself.

Would I walk out those doors like a dog forced outside for the first time? With my leash unclipped, how would I act?

Would I run?

Seek out affection?

Fight?

I was tired of fighting.

I stepped into the sun and lifted my hand to shield my tender eyes. Even that big yellow globe reminded me of my captivity. Of Marcy. I looked into it when I wanted it to incinerate me. Burn me up until I was part of the earth that held so many damn secrets.

A car horn rang out. A deep red SUV idled at the curb. I noticed the blonde hair before anything else. I hyper focused on it. The same dog who found freedom discovered something it wanted. That it'd run for.

I jogged to the car and her expression changed—not from fear or lack of recognition, but from surprise. Her lips drew up. "You look like shit," she teased.

I shook my head. Her humor got me through my worst nights. In that home *and* locked away in prison.

"You too," I said as I rubbed my hand along the car's slick metal. I climbed inside and threw my bag behind me.

She glanced over at me. Her hair had grown quite a bit, and she'd evened out the choppy pieces, but the scars of captivity remained prominent on her skin. Mine did too. They linked us, tethering us to our painful memories. Even so, I've never seen a more beautiful human being in my life.

I didn't know how to act. What to do with her. I remembered the passion as I fucked her. The way her soul merged with mine. But after ten months . . . would our souls remember each other?

Once we left that house, I didn't touch her again. I rubbed my hand along the scars created by desperate nails raking my skin as she begged me not to turn myself in, but I held too much guilt to live in society without facing the things I did. She sobbed as the police put me in the car. They comforted her, believing the tears were from the trauma she endured in captivity. They didn't realize they were for her captor.

Mackenzie threw the car in drive and we took off toward wherever she planned on taking us. No words passed between us. I'd be lying if I said there wasn't a growl within me after ten months without her. The way her chest rose with every breath . . . fuck. I had to look away from her.

What would happen when I couldn't force my focus on the passing trees and I had to face her? Truly face her? I looked at the drivers in the cars around us and remembered I never had the chance to learn to drive—or even ride down the road in the daytime—for over a decade. I never finished school. Never worked. What the fuck could I possibly offer a girl like Mackenzie?

I was an anchor.

We pulled into the parking lot of an apartment complex. She cleared her throat and got out, expecting me to follow. I hesitated, wondering if being in the same room as her was the best idea. I didn't have much of a choice. She signed a paper stating I could stay with her, and without that, the court wouldn't have granted my parole. I had to have a home to go to, even if it meant with the person I feared I would hurt.

She came to my side of the car and opened the door. "Shell shocked?" she asked.

I nodded. I'd go with that. I'd let her believe it was from being free instead of fearing I'd become Benjamin again. Fearing I'd detonate and take her body with me.

When I caught her gaze, she smiled—a naive and trusting smile she needed to wipe off her face. I didn't know if I could be trusted, and she sure as shit shouldn't trust me.

When I rose from my seat and stood in front of her—towering over her small frame more than I had before—she threw herself against my chest. I took in her scent. She smelled clean, yet familiar. I held my hands at my sides for several heartbeats before I wrapped my arms around her. She released a soft, comforted sigh, as if she'd been holding her breath until then.

Growl.

The beast inside me stirred awake and paced the perimeter. My thoughts went to places that should have died with Marcy. I stiffened, and she backed away. I covered my erection the best I could, but it was obvious. She bit her perfect fucking lip.

Don't.

I wanted to scream the word at her. I needed her to stop flirting or trying to make a move. When my cock got hard, I lost my senses, and she needed to understand that. It loosened the leash on the thrashing animal inside me.

"Come on, Dylan." She motioned forward, and I followed her to the apartment.

She unlocked the door, flipped on the light, and I looked around the quaint space.

"You didn't move back home with your parents?" I asked.

"I did for the first six months, but I was trapped in a different way there. They walked on eggshells around me. They felt my fear for me, and I couldn't stand it."

I swallowed hard. I saw my family for a moment during my trial. I recognized my mother in the rows of seats behind me. I hadn't reached out to them. They were excited to know I was alive, but that changed as the judge read my charges aloud. My mother ran off, crying. How could I hurt so many people, even ones outside that house?

"I bought some clothes for you, but I'm not sure if the shirts will fit you anymore," she said as she took me in. She drew her legs together.

My hands trembled at the tone of her voice. How was she still attracted to me after everything I did? It fucked with my head. Therapy allowed me to see myself for who I really was, and that person shouldn't have made her thighs clench.

Her eyes softened. "Talk to me."

"I don't know what you want me to say, Mackenzie."

"Tell me you didn't forget about me," she whispered.

I could *never* forget Mackenzie. I could never let go. She was ingrained in my heart. She changed my life. I loved her. I was torn between telling her we can't be what she wants us to be and telling her to close the inch of space between us. But I couldn't bring myself to push her away.

"I could never forget you, mouse."

Her lips tightened. I didn't think about how the nickname might send memories crashing into the front of her mind. Her cheeks flushed. She dropped her gaze and threw it back at me, swallowing hard.

I fucked up. Oh, I fucked—

She stepped into me, and her arms wrapped around my neck.

No, don't, I pleaded in my head as her lips inched closer to mine. I shook my head and grabbed her shoulders, holding her away from me.

"We can't," I said.

I wanted to. Fuck, I wanted to. But I didn't want to hurt her. Ten months without any kind of intimacy and then being thrust back into her world . . . it was too risky.

If I couldn't trust myself, she shouldn't either. I refused to test my willpower on her body.

Mackenzie

Rejection hurts, no matter what circumstance surrounds it. He held me away from him. His chest rose as if he were fighting what he wanted—what he knew he shouldn't want. My body recognized him, even if my eyes couldn't. He looked like a new man. The scars were the only familiar landmarks on his body.

I'd been through hell. I met the devil, and Benjamin killed it. The only thing that kept me going in that house was him. I needed him then like I still needed him now.

"Please don't . . ." I whispered. I couldn't handle his rejection.

I met the beast within him. I stared it down and stroked its grizzly coat. I heard the growls of protest every time he didn't take me against my will. When I gave myself to him, it was by choice. It was *my* choice. And I was making the choice again.

I'd risk it.

I'd push him.

I'd sacrifice myself.

I took a deep breath, grabbed the hem of my shirt, and tugged it over my head.

"Don't, mouse," he commanded, but his eyes were locked on my chest.

I stared at him as I reached back and unclipped my bra, dropping the straps off my shoulders and letting it fall to the floor. His lip trembled. His hands balled into fists at his side.

"Are you trying to get me put back in jail?"

Of course not. I knew he wouldn't hurt me. Not like he thought he would.

He bit into his lower lip until a drop of blood slipped past the seam of his mouth. I started to unbutton my jeans, but his hand reached out and wrapped around my wrist. I whimpered against his powerful grip.

"You don't know what you're doing to me," he growled. His eyes fell down my chest, stopping at the curves of my breasts.

"I do know," I whispered. "I know you."

He stepped into me. His hand wrapped around my throat without squeezing. He dragged it toward my chest. "You don't know me, mouse. Not really. You know who I let you meet."

"You won't hurt me."

"Oh, I'll fucking hurt you, and that's the problem. That's what you don't understand." He squeezed my wrist harder. "I won't be able to get enough of you if I'm allowed inside you again. Stop being stupid."

I stifled the heat behind my eyes. "I need you. In so many ways." A single tear slid down my cheek. "I need to know that everything we had was real. That I made the right choice." My lip trembled. "That I'm still yours."

His head cocked, and his grasp loosened on my wrist. "You will *always* be mine. And that's why I have to protect you."

"Then let me be yours."

He growled and tugged me into him. His hand ran down my bare back, tracing the length of my spine. My breasts pressed against his shirt. He tugged down my jeans and gripped my ass.

"Is this what you want?" Frustration laced his words.

I nodded.

"It's been ten fucking months since I've been inside you."

He was the last person I was with, too. Ten months that made me feel vacant. Like I lost my best friend.

"If I kiss you, I won't be able to stop," he said in a breathy voice.

I leaned in and let my lips find his before he could argue again. His kiss relayed his passion, and as he lifted me up, I realized just how much healthier he was. Stronger. So goddamn strong. I sucked in a quick breath of fear and hesitation. I exhaled, letting it blow away from me. I trusted him. I had to.

He carried me to the bedroom. I left the light on when I'd rushed to pick him up. I hadn't made the bed, and a moment of embarrassment washed over me as he placed me among the mess of blankets. We'd never had sex in a bed.

The memory foam conformed to my body as his weight pressed me deeper into the mattress. His hand groped my chest and rushed toward my stomach. He sat up on his knees and helped me tug my jeans the rest of the way down. The familiar darkness that overcame him before he wanted to hurt me passed over his eyes. His touch was firm, but he wasn't trying to hurt me.

His hand worked off his jeans, and he pulled himself from his boxers. He leaned over me, snaked his hand behind my neck, and drew my mouth to his. His hips pressed forward until his cock was inside me again. I gasped, but he didn't slow down or stop. He just drove his hips deeper, pushing me further into the mattress.

"Dylan," I panted.

He swallowed hard as he met my gaze. "Am I hurting you?" he asked.

He was. But I shook my head. I wanted to feel the pain.

His pain. I wanted to feel anything more than the numbness I felt for the last ten months. He growled and thrust until I felt like he was going to tear me in half. But I didn't want him to stop. He tore me in half and stitched me back together long before this.

"I can't last with you," he whispered. "You feel fucking amazing. Better than ten months of fantasizing about this moment. I never expected to be inside you again. I thought I'd always be chasing the way you made me feel." His mouth fell to mine again. "I love you, mouse," he whispered against my lips.

I didn't expect those words. I expected the pain. The passion. The frustration. But I looked up at him and realized that only love could truly tame a beast.

"I love you, and everything inside you that makes you want to hurt me," I said as I stared up at him. "Because I know against everything you were taught, everything you experienced, I'm the hand that feeds your beast."

He was everything that was wrong with my world. The embodiment of suffering. Yet when he came inside me, everything felt right. I was whole again.

If you like dark and depraved stories like this one, check out *Captured*, another dark captive/captors horror romance.
Books2read.com/CapturedBook

If you like depraved forced-proximity stories with a little more spice, check out *Hitched*.
Books2read.com/Hitched

Keep in Touch

Sign up for my newsletter and get VIP (free and first) access to my spicy novellas and other bonus content.

Acknowledgments

Thank you to my husband for continuing to support me through this journey.

I appreciate the fans I have who will hopefully still love me after they read this!

Big thank you to my editor, Sugar Free Editing, for editing my darkest story to date.

Also by Lauren Biel

To view Lauren Biel's complete list of books, visit: Campsite.bio/LaurenBielAuthor or LaurenBiel.com

About the Author

Lauren Biel is an author with several titles in the works. When she's not working, she's writing. When she's not writing, she's spending time with her husband, her friends, or her pets. You might also find her on a horseback trail ride or sitting beside a waterfall in Upstate New York. When reading her work, expect the unexpected.

To be the first to know about her upcoming titles, please visit www.LaurenBiel.com.

Printed in Great Britain
by Amazon

45768274R00138